CHILDREN'S THRIFT CLASSICS

The Prince and the Pauper

MARK TWAIN

Adapted by Bob Blaisdell
Illustrated by Thea Kliros

DOVER PUBLICATIONS, INC.
Mineola, New York

DOVER CHILDREN'S THRIFT CLASSICS
EDITOR OF THIS VOLUME: CANDACE WARD

Copyright

Published in Canada by General Publishing Company, Ltd., 30 Lesmill Road, Don Mills, Toronto, Ontario.

Bibliographical Note

This Dover edition, first published in 1997, is a new abridgment, by Bob Blaisdell, of a standard edition of the text first published in Boston by James R. Osgood & Co., 1882. The illustrations have been prepared specially for this edition.

Library of Congress Cataloging-in-Publication Data

Twain, Mark, 1835–1910.
The prince and the pauper / Mark Twain ; adapted by Bob Blaisdell ; illustrated by Thea Kliros.
p.   cm. — (Dover children's thrift classics)
Summary: When young Edward VI of England and a poor boy who resembles him exchange places, each learns something about the other's very different station in life.
ISBN 0-486-29383-1 (pbk.)
1. Edward VI, King of England, 1537–1553—Juvenile fiction. [1. Edward VI, King of England, 1537–1553—Fiction. 2. Mistaken identity—Fiction. 3. Adventure and adventurers—Fiction. 4. England—Fiction.] I. Blaisdell, Robert. II. Kliros, Thea, ill. III. Title. IV. Series.
PZ7.C584Pr   1997
[Fic]—dc20   96-9804
                                                                                 CIP
                                                                                  AC

Manufactured in the United States of America
Dover Publications, Inc., 31 East 2nd Street, Mineola, N.Y. 11501

Contents

Preface

I will set down a tale as it was told to me by one who had it of his father, who had it of *his* father, this last having in the same way had it of *his* father—and so on, back and still back, three hundred years and more, the fathers passing it on to the sons and so preserving it. It may be history, it may be only legend. It may have happened, it may not have happened: but it *could* have happened.

THE AUTHOR

Chapter 1

The Birth of the Prince and the Pauper

IN THE ANCIENT CITY of London, on a certain fall day in the second quarter of the sixteenth century, a boy was born to a poor family of the name of Canty, who did not want him. On the same day another English child was born to a rich family of the name of Tudor, who did want him. All England wanted him too. England had so longed for him, and hoped for him, and prayed God for him, that, now that he was really come, the people went nearly mad for joy. Everybody took a holiday, and high and low, rich and poor, feasted and danced and sang; and they kept this up for days and nights together. By day, London was a sight to see, with bright banners waving from every balcony and house-top, and splendid parades. By night, it was again a sight to see, with its great bonfires at every corner, and its troops making merry around them. There was no talk in all England but of the new baby, Edward Tudor, Prince of Wales, who lay covered in silks and satins. But there was no talk about the other baby, Tom Canty, covered in his poor rags, except among the family of paupers whom he had just come to trouble with his presence.

Let us skip a number of years.

London was fifteen hundred years old, and was a great town—for that day. The streets were narrow, and crooked, and dirty, especially in the part where Tom Canty lived, which was not far from London Bridge. The houses were of wood, with the second story reaching out over the first, and the third sticking its elbows out beyond the second. The windows were small, with little diamond-shaped panes, and they opened outward, on hinges, like doors.

The house which Tom's father lived in was up a foul little pocket called Offal Court, off Pudding Lane. It was small and rickety, but it was packed full of very poor families. Canty's tribe occupied a room on the third floor. The mother and father had a sort of bed in the corner; but Tom, his grandmother, and his two sisters, Bet and Nan, had all the floor to themselves, and might sleep where they chose. There were the remains of a blanket or two, and some bundles of old straw, but these could not rightly be called beds; they were kicked into a general pile, mornings, and selections made from the mass at night.

Bet and Nan were fifteen years old—twins. They were good-hearted girls, unclean, clothed in rags, and igno-rant. Their mother was like them. But the father and grandmother were a couple of fiends. They got drunk whenever they could; then they fought each other or anybody else who came in the way; they cursed and swore always; John Canty was a thief, and his mother, a beggar. They made beggars of the children, but failed to make thieves of them. Among the people that inhabited the house was a good old priest, and he used to get the children aside and teach them right ways secretly. Father Andrew also taught Tom a little Latin, and how to read and write.

All Offal Court was just such another hive as Canty's house. Drunkenness and brawling were the order every night and nearly all night long. Yet little Tom was not unhappy. He had a hard time of it, but did not know it. It was the sort of time all the Offal Court boys had, therefore he supposed it was the correct and comfortable thing. When he came home empty-handed at night after a day of begging, he knew his father would curse him and thrash him, and that when he was done the grandmother would do it all over again; and that in the night his starving mother would slip to him any scrap or crust she had been able to save for him.

In summer, Tom only begged just enough to save himself, for the laws against begging were harsh, and the penalties heavy; so he put in a good deal of his time listening to good Father Andrew's charming old tales and legends about giants and fairies, dwarfs, genii, and enchanted castles, and gorgeous kings and princes. His head grew to be full of these wonderful things, and many a night as he lay in the dark on his straw, tired, hungry, smarting from a thrashing, he let go his imagination and soon forgot his aches in picturings to himself of the charmed life of a prince in a palace. One desire came to haunt him day and night; it was to see a real prince, with his own eyes. He spoke of it once to some of his Offal Court comrades; but they jeered him

He tramped up and down, hour after hour.

and scoffed at him so much that he kept his dream to himself after that.

Each day he would go forth in his rags and beg a few farthings, eat his poor crust, take his customary abuse, and then stretch himself upon his handful of straw, and begin again his grand dreams. His desire to look just once upon a real prince, in the flesh, grew upon him, day by day, and week by week, until at last it absorbed all other desires, and became the one passion of his life.

One rainy January day, on his usual begging tour, he tramped up and down, hour after hour, barefooted and cold, looking in at shop windows and longing for the pork-pies and other items displayed there—for to him these were foods fit for the angels; that is, judging by the smell, they were—for it had never been his good luck to own and eat one.

That night Tom reached home so wet and tired and hungry that it was not possible for his father and grandmother to see his condition and not be moved—after their fashion; so they gave him a beating at once and sent him to bed. For a long time his pain and hunger, and the swearing and the fighting going on in the building, kept him awake; but at last his thoughts drifted away to far, romantic lands, and he fell asleep in the company of jewelled and gilded princelings who lived in great palaces, and had servants bowing before them or flying to carry out their orders. And then, as usual, he dreamed *he* was a princeling himself.

But when he awoke in the morning and looked upon the wretchedness about him, his dream had its usual effect—it made worse the poverty of his surroundings. Then came bitterness, and heartbreak, and tears.

Chapter 2

Tom's Meeting with the Prince

TOM GOT UP HUNGRY, and went off hungry, but with his thoughts busy with splendors of his night's dreams. He wandered here and there, hardly noticing where he was going. People bumped him, and some gave him rough words; but it was all lost on the boy.

Tom walked into Charing Village soon, and rested himself at the beautiful cross built there by a king of earlier days; then idled down a quiet, lovely road toward a mighty and majestic palace—Westminster. Tom stared in glad wonder at the vast building, the huge stone gateway, with its gilded bars and its array of colossal granite lions. Was the desire of his soul to be satisfied at last? Here, indeed, was a king's palace. Might he not hope to see a prince now?

At each side of the gilded gate stood a living statue, that is to say, a motionless man-at-arms, clad from head to heel in shining steel armor. At a respectful distance were many country-folk, and people from the city, waiting for any chance glimpse of royalty. Splendid carriages, with splendid people in them and splendid servants outside, were arriving and leaving by several other gateways.

Poor little Tom, in his rags, approached, and was moving slowly and timidly past the guards, when all at once he caught sight through the bars of a handsome boy, tanned with outdoor sports and exercises, whose clothing was all of lovely silks and satins, shining with

Tom's eyes grew big with wonder.

jewels; at his hip a little jeweled sword and dagger; fine buskins on his feet, with red heels; and on his head a red cap, with drooping plumes fastened with a sparkling gem. Several gentlemen stood near—his servants, no doubt. Oh! he was a prince—a prince, a living prince, a real prince; and the prayer of the pauper boy's heart was answered at last.

Tom's eyes grew big with wonder. Everything gave way in his mind to one desire: that was to get close to the prince, and have a good look at him. Before he knew what he was doing, he had his face against the gate-bars. The next instant one of the soldiers snatched him away, and sent him spinning among the crowd. The soldier said: "Mind your manners, you young beggar!"

The crowd jeered and laughed; but the young prince sprang to the gate, his eyes flashing with anger, and cried out:

"How dare you treat a poor lad like that! How dare you treat the king my father's subject so! Open the gates, and let him in!"

The crowd snatched off their hats then, and shouted, "Long live the Prince of Wales!"

The soldiers opened the gates, and the little Prince of Poverty passed in to join hands with the Prince of Wealth.

Edward Tudor said, "You look tired and hungry: you have been treated ill. Come with me."

He took Tom to a room in the palace. By his command a meal was brought such as Tom had never found before except in books. The prince sent away the servants, so that his humble guest might not be embarrassed by their watching; then he sat near by, and asked questions while Tom ate.

"What is your name, lad?"

"Tom Canty, sir."

"'Tis an odd one. Where do you live?"

"In the city, sir. Offal Court, off Pudding Lane."

"Have you parents?"

"Parents have I, sir, and a grandma too—also twin sisters, Nan and Bet."

"Is your father kind to you?"

"Not more than Grandma Canty, sir."

"Fathers are alike, perhaps. Mine has a temper. He strikes with a heavy hand, yet spares me. How does your mother treat you?"

"She is good, sir, and gives me neither sorrow nor pain of any sort. And Nan and Bet are like her in this."

"How old are they?"

"Fifteen, sir."

"Do your sisters, like mine, forbid the servants to smile?"

"They? Oh, do you think, sir, that *they* have servants?"

The little prince thought a moment, then said, "And why not? Who helps them undress at night? Who dresses them when they rise?"

"No one, sir. And, besides, they have but one garment each and so wear them night and day."

"Your good Nan and Bet shall have more clothes and servants then, and soon. No, thank me not; 'tis nothing. You speak well; you have grace. Are you schooled?"

"I know not if I am or not, sir. The good priest Father Andrew taught me from his books."

"Tell me of your Offal Court. Have you a pleasant life there?"

"Yes, sir, except when one is hungry. There are puppet shows, and monkeys, and plays where the actors shout and fight till all are dead, and 'tis so fine to see, and costs but a farthing—though 'tis very hard to get the farthing, your worship."

"Tell me more."

"We lads of Offal Court battle each other with clubs sometimes."

The prince's eyes flashed. He said, "That would I not dislike. Tell me more."

"We run races, sir, to see who of us shall be fleetest."

"That would I like also. Speak on."

There did not seem to have been any change made!

"In summer, sir, we wade and swim in the canals and the river, and each ducks his neighbor, and splashes him, and dives and shouts and tumbles and—"

"It would be worth my father's kingdom to enjoy such play once! Pray go on."

"We dance and sing about the Maypole; we play in the sand; and sometimes we make mud pies, sir."

"Oh, pray, do not say more, 'tis glorious! If I could wear clothes like yours, and play in the mud once, just once, with no one to scold or prevent me, I could almost give up the crown."

"And if I could clothe myself once, sweet sir, as you are—just once—"

"Oho, would you like it? Then so shall it be. Take off your rags, and put these on, lad! It is a brief happiness, but will be not less keen for that. We will have it while we may, and change again before any come to bother us."

A few minutes later the little Prince of Wales was wearing Tom's fluttering odds and ends, and the little Prince of Poverty was tricked out in the fancy garb of royalty. The two went and stood side by side before a large mirror, and lo, a miracle: there did not seem to have been any change made! They stared at each other, then at the glass, then at each other again. At last the princeling said, "You have the same hair, the same eyes, the same voice and manner, the same form and body, the same face, that I have. If we went out naked, there is no one who could say which was you, and which the Prince of Wales. And now that I am clothed as you were, it seems I am able to feel as you did when the soldier—"

"Yes, but—"

"Peace! It was a shameful thing, and cruel!" cried the little prince, stamping his bare foot. "Stir not a step till I come again. It is a command!"

In a moment he had snatched up and put away an article of national importance that lay upon the table, and was out at the door and flying through the palace grounds in his rags, with a hot face and glowing eyes. As soon as he reached the great gates, he seized the bars, and tried to shake them, shouting: "Open! Unbar the gates!"

The soldier that had maltreated Tom obeyed; and as the prince burst through the portal, the soldier gave him a smack on the ear that sent him whirling to the road, and said, "Take that, you beggar!"

The crowd roared with laughter. The prince picked himself out of the mud, and ran at the guard, shouting, "I am the Prince of Wales! You shall hang for laying your hand upon me!"

The soldier said angrily, "Be off, you crazy rubbish!"

Here the jeering crowd closed around the poor little prince, and hustled him far down the road, hooting him, and shouting, "Make way for his royal Highness! Make way for the royal Highness!"

Chapter 3

The Prince's Troubles Begin

AFTER HOURS OF teasing, the little prince was at last deserted by the mob and left to himself far away from the palace. He looked about him now, and saw he was within the city of London—but that was all he knew. He moved on, and in a little while the houses thinned, and the passers-by were rare. He bathed his bleeding feet in a brook; rested a few moments, then passed on, and soon came upon a great space with only a few scattered houses in it, and a huge church. He recognized this church. He said to himself, "It is the ancient Grey Friars' church, which the king my father has taken from the monks and given for a home forever for poor and forsaken children, and new-named it Christ's Church. Gladly will they serve the son of him who has given so much to them—and the more so as that son is himself as poor and as forlorn as any that are sheltered here."

He was soon in the midst of a crowd of boys who were running, jumping, playing ball and leap-frog. The boys stopped their play and flocked about the prince, who said, "Good lads, say to your master that Edward Prince of Wales desires a word with him."

A great shout went up at this, and one rude fellow said, "Indeed! And are you the prince's messenger, beggar?"

With laughter, they dropped upon their knees.

"I am the prince; and it ill suits you that live upon the king my father's charity to treat me this way."

The boys laughed, and the youth who had first spoken shouted to his comrades, "Hey-ho, swine, slaves, charity boys, where are your manners? Down on your knees, all of you, and give respect to his kingly rags!"

With laughter, they dropped upon their knees and did mock honor to Edward. The prince pushed away the nearest boy with his foot, and said, "Take that, till tomorrow comes and I build a gallows for you!"

This was no joke—and the laughter stopped, and fury took its place. A dozen boys shouted, "Take him off to the horse-pond! Sick the dogs on him!"

Then followed such a thing as England had never seen before—a sacred prince hit by rude boys, and set upon and torn by dogs.

As night drew to a close that day, the prince found himself far down in the city. His body was bruised, his hands were bleeding, and his rags were all muddy. He wandered on and on, and grew so tired he could hardly drag one foot after the other. He had ceased to ask questions of anyone, since they brought him only insult instead of information.

The lights began to twinkle, it came on to rain, the wind rose, and a raw and gusty night set in. The houseless prince, the homeless heir to the throne of England, still moved on, drifting deeper into the maze of poor alleys where the swarming hives of poverty massed together.

Suddenly a great drunken ruffian collared him and said, "Out to this time of night again, and have not brought a farthing home, I'll bet! If it is so, and I don't break all the bones in your lean body, then I am not John Canty!"

The prince twisted himself loose, and said, "Oh, are you *his* father, truly? Sweet Heaven let it be so—then will you go get him and bring me back!"

"*His* father? I do not know what you mean; but I know I am *your* father—"

"Oh, do not make jokes, and do not delay!—I am tired, I am hurt, I can bear no more. Take me to the king my father, and he will make you rich beyond your wildest dreams. Believe me!—I speak no lie—put out your hand and save me! I am indeed the Prince of Wales!"

The man stared down upon the lad, then shook his head and muttered, "Gone stark mad!" and then collared him once more, and said, with a coarse laugh, "But mad or not, I and your Grandma Canty will soon find where the soft places in your bones are, or I'm not a man!"

With this he dragged the prince away, and disappeared up a front court.

Chapter 4

Tom as a Prince

TOM CANTY, left alone in the prince's room, made good use of his chance. He turned himself this way and that before the large mirror, admiring his finery; then walked away, imitating the prince's manner. Next he drew the beautiful sword, and bowed, kissing the blade, and laying it across his chest, as he had seen a noble knight do. Tom played with the jeweled dagger that hung upon his thigh; he tried each of the chairs, and thought how proud he would be if the Offal Court herd could only peep in and see him now. He wondered if they would believe the marvelous story he should tell when he got home, or if they would shake their heads, and say his overworked imagination had at last upset his reason.

At the end of half an hour it suddenly occurred to him that the prince was gone a long time; then right away he began to feel lonely; very soon he ceased to toy with the pretty things about him; he grew uneasy. Suppose someone should come, and catch him in the prince's clothes, and the prince not there to explain. Might they not hang him at once, and inquire into his case afterward? His fears rose higher and higher; he softly opened the door to the next room, resolved to fly and seek the prince, and through him, protection and release. Six handsome gentlemen servants and two

By this time the boy was on his knees.

young boy servants, clothed like butterflies, sprung to their feet, and bowed low. He stepped quickly back, and shut the door. He said, "Oh, they mock me! They will go and tell."

He walked up and down the floor, listening, and start-
ing at every small sound. Soon the door opened, and a
boy said, "The Lady Jane Grey."

The door closed, and a sweet young girl, richly
dressed, bounded toward him. But she stopped suddenly, and said, "Oh, what bothers you, my lord?"

Tom stammered out, "Ah, be kind! Truly, I am no lord,
but only poor Tom Canty of Offal Court in the city.
Please let me see the prince, and he will give me back
my rags, and let me go away unhurt. Oh, be merciful,
and save me!"

By this time the boy was on his knees.

She cried out, "Oh, my lord, on your knees?—and to
me!"

Then she fled away in fright; and Tom, in despair,
sank down, murmuring, "There is no help, there is no
hope. Now they will come and take me."

While he lay there, dreadful news was spreading
through the palace. The whisper, for it was whispered
always, flew from servant to servant, from lord to lord,
lady to lady, down all the long hallways, from story to
story, from room to room, "The prince has gone mad,
the prince has gone mad!" Soon every room had its
groups of glittering lords and ladies talking in whispers.
Shortly thereafter, a splendid official came marching by
these groups, making the announcement:

IN THE NAME OF THE KING.
Let no one listen to this false and foolish matter, upon
pain of death, nor discuss it, nor speak of it outside the
palace. In the name of the king!

The whispering ceased.

Soon there was a general buzz along the corridors, of
"The prince! See, the prince comes!"

Poor Tom came slowly walking past the low-bowing groups, trying to bow in return. Great noblemen walked upon each side of him, making him lean upon them. Behind him followed the court doctors and some servants.

Then Tom found himself in a noble room of the palace, and heard the door close behind him. Around him stood those who had come with him.

Before him, at a little distance, reclined a very large and very fat man, with a stern expression. His large head was very gray; and his whiskers were gray also. His clothing was of rich stuff, but old. One of his swollen legs had a pillow under it, and was wrapped in bandages. This stern man was the dread Henry VIII. He said—and his face grew gentle as he began to speak, "How now, my lord Edward, my prince? Have you been playing a joke on me, the good king your father, who loves you, and treats you well?"

Poor Tom was listening as well as he dazedly could, to the beginning of this speech; but when the words "me, the good king" fell upon his ear, he dropped upon his knees.

"You are the king? Then I am in trouble indeed."

These words seemed to stun the king. "Ah, I had believed the rumor untrue; but I fear me 'tis not so. Come to your father, child: you are not well."

Tom was helped to his feet, and approached the Majesty of England, trembling. The king took the frightened face between his hands, and then pressed the curly head against his chest, and patted it tenderly. He said, "Do not you know your own father, child? Break not my old heart; say you know me. You do know me, do you not?"

The king pressed the curly head against his chest.

"Yes; you are my lord the king!"

"True, true—that is fine—be comforted, do not tremble so; there is no one here who would hurt you; there is no one here who does not love you. You are better now; your dream has passed—is it not so? And you know yourself again—is it not so? You will not miscall yourself again, as they say you did a little while ago?"

"I pray to you to believe me, your grace, I did speak

the truth, my lord; for I am the lowest among your subjects, being a pauper born, and 'tis by an accident I am
here, although I did nothing blameful. I am too young to
die, and you can save me with one little word. Oh,
speak it, sir!"

"Die? Talk not so, sweet prince—peace, peace to
your troubled heart—you shall not die!"

Tom dropped upon his knees with a glad cry.

"God return to you your mercy, oh my king!" Then
springing up, he turned to the two lords in waiting, and
exclaimed, "You heard it! I am not to die!" All bowed
with respect, but no one spoke. Tom was a little confused, and turned toward the king, saying, "I may go
now?"

"Go? Surely, if you wish. But why not stay yet a little?
Where would you go?"

Tom answered, "Perhaps I made a mistake; but I
thought I was free, and so I wished to go seek again the
kennel where I was born and bred to misery, yet which
shelters my mother and my sisters, and so is home to
me; as these splendors of the palace I am not used to—
oh, please, sir, let me go!"

The king was silent for a while, and then said, with
hope in his voice, "Perhaps he is mad only upon this
one topic, and has his mind uncrazed about other matters. God let it be so! We will have a test."

Then he asked Tom a question in Latin, and Tom
answered him in the same language. The king was
delighted, and showed it. He said, "Now notice all of
you: we will test him further."

He put a question to Tom in French. Tom stood silent
a moment, then said shyly, "I have no understanding of
this language, your majesty."

The king fell back upon his couch. The attendants flew to his aid; but he waved them aside, and said, "Do not bother me—it is nothing but a faintness. Raise me! There. Come here, child. There, rest your poor troubled head upon your father's heart, and be at peace. You will soon be well; 'tis but a passing fantasy. Fear not; you'll soon be well." Then he turned toward the company; his gentle manner changed, and he said, "Listen, all of you! My son is mad; but it is not permanent. Too much study has done this, and somewhat too much confinement within the palace. Away with his books and teachers! Please him with games and sports, amuse him, so that his health returns." He raised himself higher on his couch, and went on: "He is mad; but he is my son, and England's heir; and, mad or sane, still shall he reign! And hear this, and proclaim it: whoever speaks of his madness works against the peace and order of this kingdom, and shall be sent to the gallows!"

Lord Hertford announced, "The king's will is law."

The wrath faded out of the old king's face, and he said to Tom, "Kiss me, my prince. There . . . what do you fear? Am I not your loving father?"

"You are good to me, O mighty and gracious lord."

"Now, go to your games and amusements; for my illness distresses me. I am tired, and would like to rest. Go with your uncle Hertford and your servants, and come again when I feel better."

Tom was led from the king. Once more he heard the buzz of low voices exclaiming, "The prince, the prince comes!"

He saw that he was indeed a captive now, and might remain forever shut up in this gilded cage, a friendless prince, unless God pitied him and set him free.

His old dreams had been so pleasant; but this reality was so dreary!

Tom was led to the main room of a noble suite, and made to sit down.

The Lord of St. John was announced, and after making a bow to Tom, he said, "I come upon the king's errand, concerning a matter that requires privacy. Will it please your royal highness to dismiss all that attend you here, except my lord the Earl of Hertford?"

Hertford whispered to Tom to make a sign with his hand.

Observing that Tom did not seem to know how to go on, Hertford whispered to him to make a sign with his hand. When the servants left, Lord St. John said, "His majesty commands, that for reasons of state, the

prince shall hide his madness in all ways that be within his power, till it be passed and he be as he was
before. For example, that he shall deny to no one that
he is the true prince, and heir to England's greatness;
that he shall receive that reverence due to a prince;
that he shall cease to speak to any of that lowly birth
and life his madness has conjured out of his imagination; that when any matter shall perplex him as to the
thing he should do, he shall take advice in that matter
from Lord Hertford, or my humble self. So says the
king's majesty."

Tom replied, sadly, "The king has said it. No one may
question the king's command. The king shall be
obeyed."

Then the Lady Elizabeth and the Lady Jane Grey were
announced. As the young girls passed Lord Hertford,
he said in a low voice, "I pray to you, ladies, seem not
to observe his oddness, nor show surprise when his
memory fails."

Meanwhile Lord St. John was saying in Tom's ear,
"Please, sir, keep in mind what the majesty said.
Remember all you can—seem to remember all else. Let
them not see that you are much changed from usual.
Are you willing, sir, that I remain?—and your uncle?"

Tom gave a gesture meaning yes, for he was already
learning and trying to do as well as he could, according
to the king's command.

In spite of his attempt and the help from the lords,
the conversation among the young people became awk-
ward. More than once, Tom was near to breaking down,
but a word from the Princess Elizabeth or one of the
lords saved him.

However, Tom finally stumbled. It was mentioned
that Tom was to study no more at present, and Lady
Jane exclaimed, "'Tis a pity! You were proceeding so

well. But you'll yet be graced with learning like your
father, and make yourself master of as many languages
as he, my good prince."

Elizabeth came to the rescue.

"My father!" cried Tom. "He cannot speak his own so
that any but the pigs in the sties know what he means!"

He looked up and Lord St. John's eyes warned him
from continuing. He stopped, blushed, then said, "Ah,
my malady afflicts me again, and my mind wanders. I
meant the king no disrespect."

"We know it, sir," said the Princess Elizabeth, taking his hand between her two palms; "do not trouble yourself as to that. The fault is not yours, but your illness's."

"You are a gentle comforter," said Tom, "and I thank you for it."

Time wore on pleasantly, and likewise smoothly, on the whole. Snags and sand-bars grew less and less frequent, and Tom grew more and more at his ease. When it came out that the little ladies were to go with him to the Lord Mayor's banquet in the evening, he was relieved and delighted, for he felt that he should not be friendless, now, among that number of strangers.

There was a pause now, a sort of waiting silence which Tom could not understand. He glanced at Lord Hertford, who gave him a sign—but he failed to understand that, also. Elizabeth came to the rescue, and bowed, saying, "Have we permission of the prince to go?"

Tom said, "Indeed, your ladyships can have whatever of me they like. God be with you."

When the maidens were gone, Tom turned to his keepers and said, "May it please your lordships to leave me to go into some corner and rest?"

Lord Hertford said, "So it pleases your highness, it is for you to command, it is for us to obey. That you should rest is indeed a needful thing, since you must journey to the city soon."

He touched a bell, and a boy appeared, who was ordered to ask for the presence of Sir William Herbert. This gentleman came right away, and conducted Tom to an inner room. Tom's first movement, there, was to reach for a cup of water; but another servant seized it, dropped upon one knee, and offered it to him on a gold tray.

Next the tired Tom sat down and was going to take off his boots, but another servant went down upon his knees and took them off himself. He made two or three further efforts to help himself, but being cut off by a servant each time, he finally gave up. At last he laid himself down to rest, but not to sleep, for his head was too full of thoughts and the room too full of people. He did not know how to dismiss the servants, so they stayed—to his vast regret, and theirs.

Somewhat after one o'clock, Tom was dressed for dinner. He found himself as finely clothed as before, but everything different, everything changed. He was then conducted to a spacious room, where a table was set for one person. The room was half-filled with noble servants. A chaplain said grace, and Tom was about to fall to eating, but was interrupted by the lord Earl of Berkeley, who fastened a napkin about his neck. Tom's cupbearer was present, and prevented all Tom's attempts to help himself to wine. The Taster to his highness the Prince of Wales was there also, prepared to taste any suspicious dish, and run the risk of being poisoned. The Lord Chief Butler was there, and stood behind Tom's chair, overseeing the meal, under the command of the Lord Great Steward and the Lord Head Cook, who stood near. Tom had three hundred and eighty-four servants besides these; but they were not all in that room, of course; neither was Tom aware yet that they existed.

All those that were present had been well drilled to remember that the prince was temporarily out of his head, and to be careful to show no surprise at his actions.

Poor Tom ate with his fingers mainly; but no one smiled at it, or even seemed to observe it. He inspect-

Poor Tom ate with his fingers mainly.

ed his napkin, for it was of a very dainty and beautiful fabric; then he said, "Pray take it away, so that I do not accidentally get it dirty."

The Hereditary Diaperer took it away without word or protest.

Tom examined the turnips and the lettuce with interest, and asked what they were, and if they were to be eaten; for it was only recently that men had begun to raise these things in England in place of importing them as fancy foods from Holland. His question was answered with respect, and no surprise shown. When he had finished his dessert, he filled his pockets with nuts; but nobody appeared to be aware of it, or disturbed by it.

His meal being ended, a lord came and held before him a broad, shallow, golden dish with fragrant rose-water in it, to cleanse his mouth and fingers with; and my lord the Hereditary Diaperer stood by with a napkin for his use. Tom gazed at the dish a puzzled moment or two, then raised it to his lips, and took a drink. Then he returned it to the waiting lord, and said, "Nay, I like it not, my lord: it has a pretty flavor, but it lacks strength."

By his own request, our small friend was now conducted to his private room, and left there alone. He remembered the nuts he had brought away from dinner, and the joy it would be to eat them with no crowd to eye him, and no Grand Hereditaries to pester him with service; so he was soon cracking nuts, and feeling almost naturally happy for the first time since he had been made a prince. When the nuts were all gone, he stumbled upon some books in a closet, among them one about the etiquette of the English court. This was a prize. He lay down upon a sofa, and proceeded to instruct himself. Let us leave him there for the moment.

About five o'clock King Henry VIII awoke out of an unrefreshing nap, and muttered to himself, "Troublous dreams! My end is now at hand: so say these warnings, and my failing pulses confirm it."

His attendants seeing that he was awake, one of them asked his pleasure concerning the Lord Chancellor, who was waiting.

"Admit him!" exclaimed the king.

The Lord Chancellor entered, and knelt by the king's couch, saying, "I have given order, and, according to the king's command, the peers now stand at the House, where, having confirmed the Duke of Norfolk's doom, they humbly wait his majesty's further pleasure in the matter." .

The king's face lit up, and he said, "I myself will go before my Parliament, and with my own hand will I seal the warrant that rids me of—"

His voice failed, and his attendants eased him back upon his pillows. Soon he said, "Alas, let others do this for me, since 'tis denied to me. I put my Great Seal in commission: you choose the lords that shall compose it, and get to work. Hurry! Before the sun shall rise and set again, bring me his head so that I may see it."

"According to the king's command, so shall it be. Will it please your majesty to order that the Seal be now restored to me, so that I may go upon the business?"

"The Seal! Who keeps the Seal but you?"

"Please your majesty, you took it from me two days ago."

"Why, truly I did: I do remember it. . . . What did I do with it? . . . I am very feeble. . . . So often these days my memory plays tricks on me."

Lord Hertford knelt and offered, "Sire, if that I may be so bold, several of us remember that you gave the Great Seal into the hands of his highness the Prince of Wales—"

"True, most true!" interrupted the king. "Fetch it! Go: time flies!"

Lord Hertford flew to Tom, but returned to the king before very long, troubled and empty-handed. "It grieves me, my lord the king, to bear so heavy and unwelcome news; but it is the will of God that the prince's madness remains, and he cannot recall to mind that he received the Seal—"

A groan from the king interrupted the lord. After a little while his majesty said, with deep sadness, "Trouble him no more, poor child. The hand of God lies heavy upon him, and my heart goes out in loving compassion for him, and sorrow that I may not bear his burden on my own shoulders, and so bring him peace. But now, use the small Seal which before I used to take with me abroad. And remember, come no more till you do bring the Duke of Norfolk's head."

Chapter 5

The Trapped Prince

WE LEFT JOHN CANTY dragging the prince into Offal Court, with a noisy and delighted mob at his heels. There was but one person in it who offered a word for the captive, and he was not listened to. The prince continued to struggle for freedom, and to rage against the treatment he was suffering, until John Canty lost what little patience was left in him, and raised his oak club in a sudden fury over the prince's head. The single pleader for the lad sprang to stop the man's arm, and the blow fell on his own wrist. Canty roared, "You'll meddle, will you? Then have your reward."

His club crashed down upon the meddler's head: there was a groan, his form sank to the ground among the feet of the crowd, and the next moment it lay there in the dark alone.

Soon the prince found himself in John Canty's abode, with the door closed against the outsiders. By the dim light of a candle, he made out the main features of the loathsome den, and also of the people in it. Two dirty girls and a middle-aged woman cowered against the wall in one corner. From another corner came a withered hag, with streaming gray hair and evil eyes. John

Canty said to her, "Wait! There's a good show here. Don't strike him yet. Come on, now, lad, say your foolery again. Name your name. Who are you?"

"I am Edward, Prince of Wales."

"'Tis ill-breeding in such a person as you to command me to speak. I tell you now, as I told you before, I am Edward, Prince of Wales."

The stunning surprise of this reply nailed the hag's feet to the floor where she stood, and almost took away her breath. She stared at the prince in stupid amazement, which so amused her son that he burst into a roar of laughter. But the effect upon Tom Canty's mother and sisters was different. They ran forward, exclaiming, "O poor Tom, poor lad!"

The mother fell on her knees before the prince, put her hands upon his shoulders, and said, "O my poor boy! Your foolish reading has done its work at last, and taken away your wits. Ah, why did you stick to it when I warned you against it? You've broke your mother's heart."

The prince looked into her face, and said gently, "Your son is well, and has not lost his wits, good woman. Comfort yourself: let me go to the palace where he is, and right away will the king my father restore him to you."

"The king your father! O my child, shake off this dream. Call back your poor wandering memory. Look upon me. Am I not your mother that bore you, and loves you?"

The prince shook his head, and said, "God knows I do not want to grieve you, but truly I have never seen your face before."

Nan said to her father, "If you will but let him go to bed, father, rest and sleep will heal his madness: please, do."

"Do, father," said Bet.

A sounding blow upon the prince's shoulder from Canty's broad palm sent him staggering into Mrs. Canty's arms, who clasped him to her breast and sheltered him from a pelting rain of smacks and slaps.

The frightened girls retreated to their corner; but the grandmother stepped forward to assist her son. The prince sprang away from Mrs. Canty, exclaiming, "You will not suffer for me, madam. Let these swine do their will upon me alone."

Between Canty and his mother they struck the boy
many blows, and then gave the girls and their mother a
beating for showing sympathy for the victim.

"Now," said Canty, "to bed, all of you. The entertainment has tired me."

The light was put out, and the family retired. As soon
as the snorings of the head of the house and his mother showed that they were asleep, the young girls crept
to where the prince lay, and covered him tenderly from

They covered him tenderly with straw and rags.

the cold with straw and rags; and their mother crept to him also, and stroked his hair, and cried over him. She had saved a morsel for him to eat, also; but the boy's pains had swept away all appetite. He was touched by her brave and costly defense of him; and he thanked her in very noble and princely words, and begged her to go to her sleep. He added that the king his father would not let her loyal kindness and devotion go unrewarded. This return of his "madness" broke her heart, and she strained him to her breast again and again and then went back, drowned in tears, to her bed.

Utter weariness at last sealed his eyes in a deep and restful sleep. Hour after hour slipped away, and still he slept. When he woke with a start, he felt his bruises, and saw the foul straw upon which he had slept, and moaned, "Alas, it was no dream, then!"

There were several raps upon the door. John Canty ceased from snoring and said, "Who knocks? What do you want?"

A voice answered, "Do you know who it was you struck with a club?"

"No. I neither know, nor care."

"Maybe you'll change your mind soon. If you would like to save your neck, nothing but flight may help you. The man is this moment giving up the ghost. 'Tis the priest, Father Andrew!"

"God-a-mercy!" exclaimed Canty. He roused his family, and commanded, "Get up and fly—or stay where you are and die!"

Scarcely five minutes later the Canty household were in the street and flying for their lives. John Canty held the prince by the wrist, and hurried him along the dark way, giving him this caution in a low voice, "Mind your tongue, you mad fool, and do not speak our name."

He then growled these words to the rest of the family, "If it so happens that we are separated, let each make for London Bridge; then will we flee into Southwark together."

At this moment, they burst suddenly out of darkness into light, and into the middle of a crowd of singing, dancing, and shouting people, massed together on the river front. There was a line of bonfires stretching as far as one could see, up and down the Thames river; London Bridge was lit up; the entire river was aglow with the flash and shine of colored lights; and constant explosions of fireworks filled the skies.

In surprise, John Canty let go his grip on the prince for a second, and Edward wasted no time, but dived among the forest of legs about him and disappeared.

Within moments, the prince felt safe and free of Canty. He quickly realized another thing, too: that a false Prince of Wales was being feasted by the city! He concluded that the pauper lad, Tom Canty, had deliberately taken advantage of his opportunity and become the prince himself!

Therefore, there was but one thing to do—find his way to the celebration and make himself known.

While Tom Canty was sitting in a high seat in a fabulous hall, watching a parade of foreign noblemen, the real Prince of Wales was proclaiming his rights and his wrongs, denouncing the imposter prince, and demanding admission at the gates of Guildhall. The crowd outside enjoyed this show, and pressed forward and craned their necks to see the small protester. Soon they began to taunt him and mock at him, purposely to make him more furious. Tears came to his eyes, but he exclaimed, "I tell you again, you pack of dogs, I am the Prince of Wales! And all alone and friendless as I am, yet I will not be driven from my ground!"

"Though you are the prince or not, 'tis all one to me, for you are a gallant lad, and not friendless! Here I stand by your side to prove it; and know that you might have a worse friend than Miles Hendon. Rest your jaw, my child. I talk the language of these dogs like a native."

The speaker was tall and muscular. His clothes were of rich material, but faded and threadbare; the feather in his hat was broken; at his side he wore a long sword in a rusty sheath. The words of this man were received with an explosion of jeers and laughter. Some cried, "'Tis another prince in disguise!" Another said, "Take the lad from him—toss him in the horse-pond!"

Instantly a hand was laid upon the prince; as instantly the stranger's long sword was out and the meddler fell to the ground. The next moment a number of voices shouted, "Kill the dog!" And the mob closed in on the warrior, who backed himself against a wall and began to lay about him with his long weapon like a madman. His victims sprawled this way and that. The bold stranger caught up the prince in his arms and soon hurried the boy and himself far away from danger and the crowd.

Let us go into the Guildhall. Suddenly, high above the happy roar and thunder of the celebration, broke the clear peal of a bugle. There was instant silence—a deep hush; then a single voice rose—that of a messenger from the palace—and began to pipe forth a proclamation, the whole crowd standing, listening. The closing words were:

"The king is dead!"

The people all bent their heads for a few moments; then all sunk upon their knees, stretched out their hands toward Tom, and in a mighty shout said:

"Long live the king!"

Poor Tom's eyes wandered over this spectacle. Then

The stranger caught up the prince in his arms.

he looked at the Earl of Hertford, and said, in a low tone, "Answer me truly. If I uttered now a command, would such a commandment be obeyed?"

"You are the king—your word is law."

"Then shall the king's law be the law of mercy, from this day, and never more be the law of blood! Up from your knees and go to the Tower and say the king commands the Duke of Norfolk shall not die!"

The words were caught and carried from lip to lip far and wide over the hall, and as Lord Hertford hurried away, another shout burst forth:

"The reign of blood is ended! Long live Edward, king of England!"

Chapter 6

The Prince and His Deliverer

As soon as Miles Hendon and the little prince were clear of the mob they struck down through back lanes and alleys toward the river. Their way was clear until they approached London Bridge; then they plowed into the mob again, Hendon keeping a tight grip upon the prince's—no, the king's—wrist. The tremendous news was already out, and the boy learned it from a thousand voices at once—"The king is dead!" The tears sprung to his eyes and blurred his sight. Then another cry shook the night: "Long live King Edward the Sixth!" and this made his eyes light up, and thrilled him. "Ah," he thought, "how grand and strange it seems—I AM KING!"

Our friends threaded their way slowly through the crowds upon the Bridge.

Hendon's lodgings were in the little inn on the Bridge. As he neared the door with his small friend, a rough voice said, "So, you've come at last! You'll not escape again, I swear; and if pounding your bones to a pudding can teach you a lesson, you'll not keep us waiting another time, maybe"—and John Canty reached out to seize the boy.

42

Miles Hendon stepped in the way, and said, "Not so fast, friend. You are needlessly rough, I think. What is the lad to you?"

"If it's any business of yours to meddle in others' affairs, he is my son."

"'Tis a lie!" cried the little king. "I do not know him, I loathe him, and will die before I go with him."

"Then 'tis settled, and there is nothing more to say," said Hendon.

"We will see as to that!" exclaimed John Canty.

"If you even touch him, you living rubbish, I will run you through!" said Hendon, laying his hand upon his sword handle. Canty drew back. "Now know this," continued Hendon, "I took this lad under my protection when a mob of such as you would have maybe killed him; do you imagine I will desert him now to you?—for whether you are his father or not—and I think you are lying—I tell you to go your way, and be quick about it."

John Canty moved off, muttering threats and curses, and was swallowed from sight in the crowd. Hendon now went up three flights of stairs to his room, with the king, after ordering a meal to be sent there. It was a poor apartment, with a shabby bed and some odds and ends of old furniture in it, and was dimly lighted by a couple of sickly candles. The little king dragged himself to the bed and lay down upon it, almost exhausted with hunger and weariness. He had been on his feet a good part of a day and a night, for it was now almost two or three in the morning, and had eaten nothing. He murmured, "Call me when the table is spread," and sunk into a deep sleep.

Hendon smiled, and said to himself, "The little beggar takes to one's quarters and takes over one's bed with as natural and easy a way as if he owned them. In his ravings he called himself the Prince of Wales, and he keeps up that game. Poor little friendless boy, doubt-less his mind has been disordered. Well, I will be his friend; I have saved him, and already I love the bold-tongued little rascal. I will teach him, I will cure his madness; yes, I will be his elder brother, and care for him and watch over him."

He looked about for an extra blanket, but finding none, took off his cloak and wrapped the lad in it. Then Hendon walked up and down the room, talking to him-self, "If my father lives still, after these seven years that I have heard nothing from home in my foreign dungeon, he will welcome the poor lad and give him generous shelter for my sake; so will my good elder brother, Arthur; my other brother, Hugh—I will crack his crown, if he interferes, the fox-hearted animal. Yes, to Hendon Hall will we go—and right away, too."

A servant entered with a hot meal, set it upon a small table, and left. The door slammed after him, and the noise woke the boy, who sprung up and looked about him. He noticed Miles Hendon's cloak around him—glanced from that to Hendon, and said, "You are good to me. Take it and put it on—I shall not need it more."

Then he got up and walked to the washstand in the corner, and stood there waiting. Hendon said in a cheery voice, "We'll have a right hearty supper now, for everything is smoking hot, and that and your nap will make you a little man again, never fear!"

The boy made no answer, but bent a steady look upon the knight. Hendon was puzzled, and said, "What's the matter?"

"Good sir, I would like to wash."

"Oh, is that all! Ask no permission of Miles Hendon for anything you like. Make yourself perfectly free here and welcome with all that belongs to me."

Still the boy stood, and did not move; he tapped the floor with his foot. Hendon was perplexed. He said, "Bless us, what is it?"

He took his stand behind the king.

"Please, pour the water, and stop talking so much!" Hendon wanted to laugh, but said to himself, "Isn't this something!" and went forward and did the small rude one's bidding; then stood by, until the command, "Come—the towel!" woke him up. He took up a towel from under the boy's nose and handed it to him. His adopted child seated himself at the table and prepared to eat. Hendon drew back the other chair and was about to place himself at the table, when the boy said:

"Halt! Would you sit in the presence of the king?"

Hendon muttered to himself, "The poor thing's madness is up with the time! It has changed with the great change that has come to England, and now in his fancy he is *king!* I must humor him!"

He removed the chair from the table, took his stand behind the king, and proceeded to wait upon him in the courtliest way he was capable of.

When the king ate, his dignity relaxed a little and with his growing contentment came a desire to talk. He said, "I think you called yourself Miles Hendon?"

"Yes, sire," Miles replied; then said to himself, "If I *must* humor the poor lad's madness, I must sire him, I must majesty him."

The king said, "I would like to know about you—tell me your story. You have a gallant way with you. Are you nobly born?"

"We are the tail of the nobility, your majesty. My father is a baronet—one of the smaller lords—Sir Richard Hendon, of Hendon Hall, in Kent."

"The name has escaped my memory. Go on."

"My father, Sir Richard, is very rich, and generous. My mother died when I was yet a boy. I have two brothers: Arthur, my elder, with a soul like his father's; and Hugh, younger than I, a mean-spirited reptile. Such was he from the cradle; such was he ten years past, when I last saw him—a ripe rascal at nineteen, I being twenty then, and Arthur twenty-two. There is none other of us but the Lady Edith, my cousin—she was sixteen then—beautiful, gentle, good, the daughter of an earl, heiress of a great fortune. My father was her guardian. I loved her and she loved me; but she was engaged to Arthur from the cradle, and Sir Richard would not allow the marriage contract to be broken. Arthur loved another maid, and told us to hope that luck would some day give us what we wanted. My father loved Hugh best of all; Hugh talked much of my faults and made them seem crimes. Then he put a silken ladder in my rooms, and convinced my father that I meant to carry off my Edith and marry with her, in defiance of his wish, and Sir Richard believed him.

"Three years of banishment from home and England might make a soldier and man of me, my father said, and teach me some wisdom. I fought out my long period in the continental wars, tasting deeply of hard knocks and adventure; but in my last battle I was taken captive, and during the seven years since then, a foreign dungeon has held me. Through wit and courage I won my escape, and fled here; and I am just arrived, poor in money and clothes, and poorer still in the knowledge of what these seven years have brought to Hendon Hall. So, sir, my tale is told."

"You have been shamefully abused!" said the little king. "But I will set things right—I swear to it! The king has said so."

Then, fired by the story of Miles's wrongs, he poured out the history of his own recent misfortunes. When he had finished, Miles said to himself, "What an imagination!"

The king went on, "You saved me from injury and shame, and perhaps even saved my life, and so my crown. Such service demands rich reward. Name your desire, and if it is within the compass of my royal power, it is yours."

Hendon was about to thank the king and put the matter aside with saying he had only done his duty and desired no reward, but a wiser thought came into his head, and he dropped upon one knee and said, "My poor service went not beyond the limit of a subject's duty, but since your majesty is pleased to hold it worthy of some reward, I ask this: that I and my heirs may have and hold the privilege of being allowed to *sit* in the presence of the majesty of England!"

"Rise, Sir Miles Hendon, knight," said the king, "rise and seat yourself. Your petition is granted. While England remains, and the crown continues, the privilege shall not lapse."

Hendon dropped into a chair at the table, saying to himself, "'Twas a good thought, and has brought me a mighty deliverance; my legs are terribly tired. If I had not thought of that, I must have had to stand for weeks, till my poor lad's wits are cured."

A heavy drowsiness soon fell upon the two comrades. The king said, "Remove these rags"—meaning his clothing.

Hendon undressed the boy, tucked him into bed, and said to himself, "He has taken my bed again, as before—what shall *I* do?"

The little king saw Hendon's confusion, and said, sleepily, "You will sleep against the door, and guard it." In a moment he was in a deep slumber.

"Dear heart, he should have been born a king!" muttered Hendon. "He plays the part so well."

Then he stretched himself across the floor and dropped asleep as the dawn appeared. Toward noon, he rose, uncovered the sleeping child—a section at a time—and took his measure with a string. The king awoke just as he had completed his work, complained of the cold, and asked what he was doing.

"'Tis done now, your majesty," said Hendon; "I have a bit of business outside, but will soon return; sleep again—you need it."

The king went back to dreamland, his head under the covers, and Miles slipped out, and slipped as softly in again, in the course of thirty or forty minutes, with a complete second-hand suit of boy's clothing, of cheap material; but neat, and warm. He was saying to himself, "The inn is paid for—as is the breakfast to come—and there is enough left to buy a couple of donkeys and meet our little costs for two or three days between here and the plenty that awaits us at Hendon Hall."

He threw back the covers over the sleeping king—he was gone!

Hendon stared about him speechless for a moment; then he began to rage and shout for the innkeeper. At that moment a servant entered with the breakfast.

"Explain!" cried the knight. "Where is the boy?"

The waiter, trembling, said, "You were hardly gone from the place, sir, when a youth came running and said it was your wish that the boy come to you straight, at the bridge-end. I brought him here to the room; and when he woke the lad and gave his message, the lad grumbled, but right away put on his rags and went with the youth."

"You fool!" said Hendon. "Yet perhaps no hurt is done. Possibly no harm is meant the boy. I will go fetch him. Set the table.—But wait! Was that youth alone?"

"When he came, no one came with him; but now I remember that as the two stepped into the mob of the Bridge, a ruffian-looking man plunged out from sone near place, and just as he was joining them—"

"What then?" thundered Hendon.

"Just then the crowd lapped them up and closed them in, and I saw no more."

"Which way did they go?"

"South, sir, I believe."

Hendon ran out, and plunged down two steps at a stride, muttering, "'Twas that scurvy villain that claimed he was his son. I have lost you, my poor little mad master—and I had come to love you so! No! not lost, for I will ransack the land till I find you again." As he wormed his way through the crowds upon the Bridge, he several times said to himself, "He grumbled, but he *went*—he went, yes, because he thought Miles Hendon asked it, sweet lad—he would never have done it for another, I know that!"

Chapter 7

"The King Is Dead—Long Live the King!"

TOWARD DAYLIGHT of the same morning, Tom Canty woke up from a heavy sleep, in the dark, and burst out, "Hey, Nan! Bet! Kick off your straw and let me tell you the wildest madcap dream that ever was! . . . Hey, Nan, I say! Bet!"

A dim form appeared at his side, and a voice said, "Will you deliver your commands?"

"Commands? . . . Oh, woe is me, I know that voice! Tell me, you—who am I?"

"You? Truly, yesterday you were the Prince of Wales, today you are my most gracious Edward, king of England."

"Alas! It was no dream! Go to your rest, sir—leave me to my sorrows."

And Tom slept again. When he next opened his eyes—the richly dressed First Lord of the Bedchamber was kneeling by his couch. The poor boy recognized that he was still a captive and a king. The room was filled with messengers clothed in purple robes.

The weighty business of dressing began, and one messenger after another knelt and paid his court and offered to the little king his condolence upon his heavy

51

loss, while the dressing went on. In the beginning, a shirt was taken up by the Chief Equerry in Waiting, who passed it to the First Lord of the Buckhounds, who passed it to the Third Groom of the Stole, who passed it to the Chancellor Royal of the Duchy of Lancaster, who passed it to the Master of the Wardrobe, who passed it to Norroy King-at-Arms, who passed it to the Constable of the Tower, who passed it to the Hereditary

Each garment had to go through this slow process.

Grand Diaperer, who passed it to the Lord High Admiral of England, who passed it to the Archbishop of Canterbury, who passed it to the First Lord of the Bedchamber, who took what was left of it and put it on Tom.

Each garment in turn had to go through this slow and solemn process. But all things must have an end, and so in time Tom Canty was in condition to get out of bed. The proper official poured water, the proper official did the washing, the proper official stood by with a towel, and by and by, Tom got through the stage and was ready for the services of the Hairdresser-royal. When he at length emerged from his master's hands, he was a gracious figure and as pretty as a girl, in his cloak and trunks of purple satin, and purple-plumed cap. He now moved toward his breakfast-room, through the midst of the courtly assemblage; and as he passed, they dropped upon their knees.

After breakfast he was conducted to the throne-room, where he proceeded to do the business of state. His "uncle," Lord Hertford, took his stand by the throne, to assist the royal mind with wise counsel.

Tom nodded consent to things he did not understand, worried about large sums of money, and named dukes and earls. While he sat thinking a moment over the ease with which he was doing strange and glittering miracles, a happy thought shot into his mind: why not make his mother Duchess of Offal Court and give her an estate? But a sorrowful thought swept it instantly away; if he gave to these lords this order, they would simply listen with unbelieving ears, then send for the doctor.

In the afternoon a slim lad about twelve years of age was admitted to his presence. He advanced, head bowed and bare, and dropped upon one knee in front of Tom.

"Rise, lad. Who are you? What would you like?"

The boy rose, and said, "Surely you must remember me, my lord. I am your whipping-boy."

"My *whipping*-boy?"

"Yes, your grace. I am Humphrey Marlow."

What should Tom do?—pretend he knew this lad? No. He stroked his brow, perplexedly, a moment or two, and said, "Now I seem to remember you somewhat— but my mind is clogged and dim with suffering—"

"Alas, my poor master!" said the whipping-boy. "In truth, 'tis as they said—his mind is gone—alas, poor soul!"

"'Tis strange how my memory plays with me these days," said Tom. "But do not mind it.—Tell me your business."

"'Tis matter of small weight, yet I will touch upon it, if it please your grace. Two days ago, when your majesty faulted three times in your Greek—in the morning lessons—do you remember?"

"Ye-e-s—I think I do. Go on."

"The master, being angry with what he termed sloppy and stupid work, promised that he would soundly whip me for it—and—"

"Whip *you!*" said Tom. "Why should he whip *you* for faults of mine?"

"Ah, you forget again. He always whips me, when you fail in your lessons."

"True, true—I forgot. You teach me, then if I fail, he argues that your job was lamely done, and—"

"Oh, my king, what words are these? I, the humblest of your servants, presume to teach *you?*"

"Then where is the blame? What riddle is this? Have I gone mad, or is it you? Explain."

"But, your majesty, there's nothing that needs explanation. No one may strike the sacred Prince of Wales; therefore, when he makes mistakes, 'tis I that take them; and surely it is right, for that is my duty and my livelihood."

Tom stared at the boy, observing to himself, "What a strange and curious trade!" Then he said aloud: "And have you been beaten, poor friend, according to the promise?"

Tom encouraged Humphrey to talk.

"No, your majesty, my punishment was appointed for this day, and perhaps it may be cancelled, as unbefitting the season of mourning that is upon us."

"Set your mind at ease—your back will go un-whipped—I will see to it."

"Oh, thanks, my good lord!" cried the boy.

Tom had wit enough to see that here was a lad who could be useful to him. He encouraged Humphrey to talk, and at the end of an hour, Tom found himself well loaded with very valuable information concerning people and matters having to do with the court; so he resolved to draw instruction from the boy daily.

Humphrey had hardly been dismissed when Lord Hertford arrived with more trouble for Tom. He noticed that the king's memory had improved (where Humphrey had given him information), and so spoke up and said in a quite hopeful voice:

"Now I am persuaded that if your majesty will try to remember yet a little further, you will resolve the puzzle of the loss of the Great Seal."

Tom was at sea—a Great Seal was a something which he was totally unacquainted with. After a moment, he asked, "What was it like, my lord?"

Hertford was surprised, and muttered to himself, "Alas, his wits have flown again—it was a mistake to lead him on to strain them"—then he turned the talk to other matters.

The next day the foreign ambassadors came; and Tom received them. The splendors of the scene delighted his eye at first, but the audience was long and dreary, and so were most of the speeches. He looked enough like a king, but he was unable to feel like one. He was glad when the ceremony was ended.

The third day of Tom Canty's kingship came and went much as the others had done, but he began to feel less uncomfortable than at first; he was getting a little used to his surroundings.

On the fourth day, awaiting a great public dinner, he was conversing with the Earl of Hertford when he looked out the window and became interested in the life and movement of the great highway beyond the palace gates. He saw a hooting and shouting mob of disorderly men, women, and children approaching from up the road.

"I wish I knew what 'tis about," he exclaimed.

"You are the king," said the earl. "Have I your permission to act?"

"Oh, yes! Oh, gladly, yes!" He added to himself, "In truth, being a king is not all dreariness—it has its compensations."

A few seconds later, Hertford's messenger returned, to report that the crowd was following a man, a woman, and a young girl to execution for crimes committed against the peace of the realm.

Death—and a violent death—for these poor unfortunates!

Tom's concern made him forget, for the moment, that he was but a false king; and before he knew it he had blurted out the command:

"Bring them here!"

His order brought no sort of surprise to the earl's face or the waiting servant's. He said to himself, "Truly it is like what I used to feel when I read the old priest's tales, and imagined myself a prince, giving law and command to all, saying, 'Do this, do that,' with no one objecting."

In a little while the culprits entered his presence in charge of an under-sheriff and escorted by a detail of the king's guard. The three doomed prisoners knelt. Something about the appearance of the man had stirred a vague memory in Tom. "I think I have seen this man before now . . . but the when or the where fail me"—such was Tom's thought.

Addressing the under-sheriff, Tom said, "Good sir, what is this man's offense?"

The officer knelt and answered, "So please your majesty, he has taken the life of a subject by poison."

"The charge was proven?"

"Most clearly, sire."

The prisoner clasped his hands together, and wrung them despairingly, saying, "Oh, my lord the king, if you can pity the lost, have pity upon me! I am innocent."

Tom looked at the under-sheriff and said, "Good sir, I would look into this matter further. Tell me what you know."

"If the king's grace please, it appeared in the trial, that this man entered into a house where one lay sick— the sick man being alone at the time, and sleeping—and soon the man came out again, and went on his way. The sick man died within the hour."

"Did anyone see the poison given?" asked Tom. "Was poison found?"

"No, my king."

"Then how does one know there was poison given at all?"

"Please your majesty, the doctors testified that none die with such symptoms but by poison."

This was an argument of force in that day. Tom offered the prisoner a chance, saying, "If you can say anything in your own behalf, speak."

"Nothing that will help, my king. I am innocent, yet I cannot make it appear so. I have no friends, otherwise

I might show that I was not in that neighborhood that day; so also I might show that at the hour they named for the poisoning, I was more than three miles away. While they say I was taking a life, I was saving one. A drowning boy—"

"Peace! Sheriff, name the day the deed was done!"

"At ten in the morning, the first day of the new year, most illustrious—"

"Let the prisoner go free—it is the king's will!"

For Tom suddenly remembered that this was the stranger who had plucked Tom's comrade from Offal Court, Giles Witt, out of the Thames, and saved his life that windy, bitter first day of the new year.

A low buzz of admiration swept through the assemblage at Tom's pardon of the man.

"This is no mad king—he has sound wits," said one observer.

"This is no weakling, but a king," said another. "He has carried himself like his own father."

Now Tom was eager to know what sort of deadly mischief the woman and the girl could have been about. "What is it that these have done?"

"Please your majesty, a terrible crime is charged against them, and clearly proven; therefore the judges have decreed, according to law, that they be hanged. They sold themselves to the devil—such is their crime."

"Have they confessed?"

"Nay, sire—they deny it."

"Then, pray tell me, how was it known?"

"It is in evidence that through wicked power, they brought about a storm that wasted all the region round about."

"Certainly, this is a serious matter," said Tom. Then

he asked, "Did the woman, also, suffer from the storm?"

The sheriff answered, "Indeed she did, your majesty. Her home was swept away, and herself and the child left shelterless."

The sheriff answered, "Her home was swept away."

"If she paid with her soul to the devil for this, she must be mad; and if she is mad, she does not know what she does, therefore has not sinned."

The elderly counselors nodded in recognition of Tom's wisdom once more.

He asked the sheriff, "How did they bring about this storm?"

"By pulling off their stockings, sire."

"Amazing," said Tom. "Has it always this effect?"

"Always, my king—at least if the woman desires it, and utters the needful words."

Tom turned to the woman and said, "Exert your power—I would like to see a storm!"

Seeing a puzzled and astonished look in the woman's face, he added, "Never fear—you shall be blameless. Even more—you will go free—no one shall touch you. Exert your power."

"O my lord the king, I do not have such power—I have been falsely accused."

"Be of good heart, you shall suffer no harm. Make a storm—it does not matter how small a one—do this and your life is spared—you shall go out free, with your child, bearing the king's pardon, and safe from hurt from anyone."

The woman protested, with tears, that she had no power to do the miracle, or else she would gladly win her child's life alone, and be content to lose her own, if by obedience to the king's command so precious a grace might be obtained.

Tom urged—the woman still protested. Finally he said:

"I think the woman has spoken the truth. If my mother were in her place and had the devil's power, she would not have stopped a moment to call her storms and lay the whole land in ruins, if the saving of my life were the price! It is argued that other mothers are made in the same way. You are free, good woman—you and your child—for I think you are innocent. Now there's nothing to fear—so pull off your stockings!—if you can make a storm, you shall be rich."

The woman was loud in thanks, and proceeded to obey, while Tom looked on. The woman stripped her own feet and her little girl's also, and plainly did her best to reward the king's kindness with an earthquake, but it was all a failure. Tom sighed, and said:

"There, good soul, trouble yourself no further, your power is no more. Go your way in peace."

Chapter 8

Foo-foo the First

L ET US RETURN to the vanished little king now.

The ruffian, whom the waiter at the inn saw, fell in close behind the youth and the king and followed their steps. He said nothing. His left arm was in a sling, and he wore a large green patch over his left eye; he limped slightly, and used an oaken staff as a support. The youth led the king a crooked course through Southwark, and by and by struck into the highroad beyond. The king was irritated now, and said he would stop here—it was Hendon's place to come to him, not his to go to Hendon.

The youth said, "You'll wait here, while your friend lies wounded in the wood yonder?"

The king cried out, "Wounded? And who has dared to do this to him? Lead on, lead on!"

It was some distance to the wood, but they made their way to it and through it speedily. By and by an open place was reached, where were the charred remains of a farmhouse, and near them a barn which was falling to ruin. There was no sign of life anywhere. The youth entered the barn, the king following upon his heels. No one there!

"Where is he?" asked the king.

A mocking laugh was his answer. Another mocking laugh came from behind. It was from the lame ruffian, who had been following at a distance. The king turned and said, "Who are you? What is your business here?"

"Leave your foolery," said the man, "and quiet yourself. My disguise isn't that good that you wouldn't know your father through it."

"You are not my father. I do not know you. I am the king. If you have hid my servant, Miles Hendon, find him for me."

John Canty replied, "It is plain you are mad, and I would not like to punish you; but if you provoke me, I must. I have done a murder, and may not stay at home—neither shall you, seeing I need your help. My name is changed, for wise reasons; it is Hobbs—John Hobbs; yours is Jack. Now then, tell me, where is your mother? Where are your sisters?"

The king answered, "My mother is dead; my sisters are in the palace."

The youth near by burst into laughter, but "Hobbs" said, "Peace, Hugo, do not vex him; his mind is gone. Sit down, 'Jack,' and quiet yourself and have something to eat."

The king moved away as far as he could from them,

into the twilight of the farther end of the barn, where he found some straw, drew it over himself, and was soon sunk into a slumber.

After a long time, he awoke, wondering where he was. He heard a chorus of cackles and laughter. A grim

Around the fire sprawled gutter-scum and ruffians.

picture met his eye. A bright fire was burning in the middle of the earthen floor, at the other end of the barn; and around it, and lit up by the red glare, lolled and sprawled the motliest company of tattered gutter-scum and ruffians, of both sexes, he had ever read or dreamed of. There were huge men clothed in fantastic rags; there were middle-sized youths dressed the same; there were blind beggars, with patched or bandaged eyes; crippled ones, with wooden legs and crutches;

some of the females were hardly grown girls, some were old and wrinkled hags, and all were loud and foul-mouthed; there were three babies; there were a couple of starving dogs.

The night was come, the gang had just finished feasting, and liquor was being passed around.

One of the blind men got up, and cast aside the patches that blocked his excellent sight. One of the cripples took off his wooden leg and stood upon two healthy ones. Then he and his fellow-rascal roared out a rollicking song, and were reinforced by the whole crew, at the end of each stanza, in a rousing chorus.

Conversation followed. In the course of it, it appeared that "John Hobbs" was not a new recruit, but had trained in the gang at some time. His story was called for, and when he said he had "accidentally" killed a man, and that he had been a priest, he was roundly applauded, and had to take a drink with everybody. He was asked why he had "been away so many months."

He answered, "London is better than the country, and safer these years, the laws are so bitter and harshly enforced. If I had not had that accident, I would have stayed there."

He asked how many persons the gang numbered now. The "Ruffler," or chief, answered, "Five and twenty thieves, beggars, hussies, and marauders. Most are here, the rest are wandering eastward. We will follow at dawn."

"I do not see Wen among the honest folk about me. Where may he be?"

"Poor lad, his diet is brimstone now. He was killed in a brawl in midsummer."

"I sorrow to hear that. Have any other of our friends fared hardly?" asked Hobbs.

"Some—yes. Particularly new-comers—such as small farmers turned hungry upon the world because their farms were taken from them to be changed to sheep ranges. They begged, and were whipped till the blood ran; then set in the stocks; they begged again, were whipped again, and deprived of an ear; they begged a third time—poor devils, what else could they do?—and were branded on the cheek with a red-hot iron, then sold for slaves; they ran away, were hunted down, and hanged. Others of us have fared less hardly."

One man stood up, and said, "I am Yokel, once a farmer and well-off, with loving wife and kids—now the wife and kids are gone; maybe in heaven, maybe in the other place—but thank God no more in *England!* My good old blameless mother earned her bread by nursing the sick; one of the patients died, the doctors knew not how, so my mother was burned for a witch. English law! I begged from house to house—I and the wife—bearing with us the hungry kids—but it was a crime to be hungry in England—so they stripped us and lashed us. Drink ye all to the merciful English law! The lash killed my Mary, and she lies in the graveyard, safe from all harms. And the kids—well, they starved. I begged again—and got the stocks and lost an ear. And still I begged again, and was sold for a slave. An English slave! That is he that stands before ye. I have run from my master, and when I am found—I shall hang!"

A ringing voice came out:

"You shall not!—and this day the end of that law is come!"

All turned and saw the little ruler coming. As he emerged into the light and was clearly revealed, questions broke out:

"Who is it?—Who are you?"

The boy stood and answered with princely dignity: "I am Edward, king of England."

A wild burst of laughter followed.

The king was angry. He said sharply, "You mannerless vagrants, is this your recognition of the royal gift I have promised?"

John "Hobbs" called out, declaring, "Mates, he is my son, a dreamer, a fool, and stark mad—don't mind him—he thinks he is the king."

"I *am* the king," said Edward, turning toward him, "as you shall know, in good time. You have confessed to a murder—you shall swing for it!"

"You'll betray me!—*you?* If I get my hands on you—"

The Ruffler ordered Hobbs to be quiet, and then said to his majesty, "You must make no threats against your mates, lad; and you must guard your tongue from saying evil of them elsewhere. Be kin, if it pleases your madness, but sink the title you have uttered—'tis treason. We're bad men, but none among us is so base as to be a traitor to his king. Now—all together: 'Long live Edward, king of England!'"

"LONG LIVE EDWARD, KING OF ENGLAND!"

The little king's face lighted with pleasure for an instant, and he said, "I thank you, my good people."

This unexpected response threw the company into convulsions of merriment.

The Ruffler said then, "Amuse yourself, if you must, but choose some other title than Edward, king of England."

A thief shrieked out a suggestion, "Foo-foo the First, king of the Mooncalves!"

The title took at once, every throat responded, and a roaring shout went up, of: "Love live Foo-foo the First, king of the Mooncalves!" followed by hootings and laughter.

Almost before the poor little victim could draw a breath he was crowned with a tin basin, robed in a tattered blanket, throned upon a barrel, and sceptred with

A thief shrieked out, "Foo-foo the First!"

the tinker's soldering-iron. Then all flung themselves on their knees about him and sent up a chorus of mocking requests:

"Be gracious to us, O sweet king!"

"Pity your slaves, and comfort them with a royal kick!"

Tears of shame came to the little monarch's eyes and anger to his heart. He thought to himself, "Had I offered them a deep wrong they could not be more cruel—yet

have I offered them nothing but to do them a kindness—and it is this way they treat me for it!"

Soon after this painful moment, at early dawn, the
troop of vagabonds set forward from the barn on their
march. The Ruffler put "Jack" in Hugo's charge, with
some brief instructions, and commanded John Hobbs
to keep away from him and let the lad alone.

About noon, after a long and weary tramp, the gang
came to a halt behind a hedge on the outskirts of a
large village. An hour was allowed for rest, then the
crew scattered themselves to enter the village at different points to try their various schemes. "Jack" and
Hugo wandered hither and thither for some time, Hugo
watching for a chance to do a stroke of business but
finding none—so he finally said, "I see nothing to steal.
So where will we beg?"

"*We!* Follow your trade—it suits you. But I will not
beg."

"You'll not beg!" exclaimed Hugo. "Since when have
you reformed?"

"What do you mean?"

"Mean? Haven't you begged the streets of London all
your life?"

"I? You idiot!"

"Now, listen, mate; you will not beg, you will not rob;
so be it. But I will tell you what you *will* do. You will play
decoy while *I* beg.—Now, peace! Here comes one with a
kindly face. Now I will fall down in a fit. When the
stranger runs to me, set up a wail, and fall upon your
knees, seeming to weep; then cry out as if all the devils
of misery were in your belly, and say, 'Oh, sir, it is my
poor brother! Look upon this sick, forsaken, miserable
wretch; please give us one little penny out of your rich-
es'—and, mind you, keep on wailing, and don't stop, till
we've tricked him out of his penny."

Then immediately Hugo began to moan, and groan, and roll his eyes; and when the stranger was close, down he sprawled, with a shriek, and began to seem in agony.

"Oh dear, Oh dear!" cried the stranger. "How he suffers! There—let me help you up."

"O, noble sir, please," said Hugo, "I am in cruel pain. My brother there will tell you how I am in torment when these fits come over me. A penny, dear sir, a penny, to buy a little food; then leave me to my sorrows."

"A penny! You shall have three, you poor creature"—and he fumbled in his pocket and got them out. "There, poor lad, take them. Now come here, my boy," he said to the king, "and help me carry your brother to that house there—"

"I am not his brother," said Edward. "He's a beggar and a thief! He has got your money and has picked your pocket."

In a moment Hugo was up and off like the wind, the gentleman following after and raising a shout for help as he went. The king fled in the opposite direction and did not slow down until he was out of harm's reach. He took the first road that came, and soon put the village behind him. He hurried along, watching out over his shoulder.

Finally, the poor hungry king, traveling without stopping, faced a chilly, overcast night. He went on through fields and forests, and came to a dark barn. He found and covered himself with two dusty horse blankets and lay down in a stall. He was a glad monarch now, though the blankets were old and thin, and not quite warm enough; and besides gave out a strong horsy odor.

Although the king was hungry and chilly, he was also so tired that he soon dozed off. Then, just as he was losing himself to sleep completely, he felt something touch him! He was wide awake in a moment, and gasping for breath, his heart standing still. He lay motionless, and listened. But nothing stirred, and there was no sound. He continued to listen, and wait for a long time. So he began to drop into a drowse once more at last; and all at once he felt that mysterious touch again! It was a grisly thing, this light touch from this noiseless and invisible presence; it made the boy sick with fear. What should he do? He knew—he must put out his hand and find that thing.

It was easy to think this; but it was hard to brace himself up to try it. Three times he stretched his hand a little way out into the dark; and snatched it suddenly back, with a gasp—not because it had found anything, but because he had felt so sure it was just *going* to. But the fourth time he groped a little further, and his hand lightly swept against something soft and warm. This so frightened him he could hardly move. But his curiosity made him grope again, and his hand encountered a bunch of long hair; he shuddered, but followed up the hair and found what seemed to be a warm rope; followed up the rope and found an innocent calf!—for the rope was not a rope at all, but the calf's tail.

The king was not only delighted to find that the creature was only a calf, but delighted to have the calf's company. While stroking its sleek, warm back—for it lay near him and within easy reach—it occurred to him to rearrange his bed, spreading it down close to the calf; then he cuddled himself up to the calf's back, drew the covers up over himself and his friend, and in a minute or two was as warm and comfortable as he had ever been in the soft couches of the regal palace of Westminster.

When the king awoke in the early morning, he got up and stepped out of the stall, and just then he heard the sound of children's voices. The barn door opened and a couple of little girls came in. As soon as they saw him their talking and laughing ceased, and they stopped and gazed at him.

He cuddled himself up to the calf's back.

Then they came nearer, holding each other's hands for protection, and took a good stare. One of them plucked up all her courage and asked, "Who are you, boy?"

"I am the king," was the answer.

"The *king?* What king?"

"The king of England."

The girls looked at each other, then at him. One of them said, "Did you hear him, Margery?—he says he's the king. Can that be true?"

"How can it be anything but true, Prissy? Would he say a lie?"

Prissy said to the king: "If you are truly the king, then I believe you."

"I am truly the king."

He then told them his story, and it was a relief to him to pour out his troubles where they would not be scoffed at or doubted. When they learned how long he had been without food, they hurried him away to the farmhouse to find a breakfast for him.

The king was cheerful and happy now, and said to himself, "When I come to my power again, I will always honor little children, remembering how that these trusted me and believed me in my time of trouble; while those that were older, and thought themselves wiser, mocked at me and took me for a liar."

The children's mother received the king kindly, and was full of pity; for his condition and apparently crazed mind touched her heart.

The boy had a hearty and satisfying meal, and was greatly refreshed and gladdened by it. But when breakfast was over, the housewife told the king to wash up the dishes. This command staggered the king for a moment, but then he said to himself, "I will try it."

He made a poor job of it; and to his surprise, too, for the cleaning of wooden spoons and plates had seemed an easy thing to do. It was a slow and hard piece of work, but he finished it at last. He was becoming impatient to get away on his journey now, and he suddenly spied, out the window at the front gate, John Canty and Hugo!

He stepped quietly out the back way and was instantly collared by Canty.

A moment or two later, his captors, each gripping him by an arm, were hurrying him with all speed through the forest.

Chapter 9

Down by Law

ONCE MORE "King Foo-foo the First" was roving with the tramps and outlaws. None but Canty and Hugo really disliked him. Some of the others liked him, and all admired his pluck and spirit. All attempts to make the king serviceable to the troop, however, had failed. He had refused to act; moreover, he was always trying to escape. He was sent out, in Hugo's care, in company with a woman and a baby, to beg; but he declined to plead for the beggars.

Hugo reported the affair to the Ruffler, who listened, thought, and then decided that the king should not be again detailed to beg, since it was plain he was worthy of something higher and better—so, on the spot he promoted him from beggar to thief!

Hugo strolled off to a neighboring village with the king; and the two drifted slowly up and down one street after another, the one watching sharply for a chance to steal, and the other as sharply for a chance to dart away and get free. Hugo's chance came first. For at last a woman approached who carried a fat package of some sort in a basket. Hugo waited and watched till the woman had passed by; then he said, in a low voice,

"Wait here till I come back," and darted after the woman.

The king's heart was filled with joy—he could make his escape now, if Hugo's quest only carried him far enough away.

But he was to have no such luck. Hugo crept behind the woman, snatched the package, and came running back, wrapping it in an old piece of blanket which he carried on his arm. The cry of "Thief" was raised in a moment by the woman, although she had not seen the stealing done. Hugo thrust the bundle in the king's hands without halting.

The next moment Hugo turned a corner and darted down a crooked alley.

The king threw the bundle on the ground; and the blanket fell away from it just as the woman arrived, with a crowd at her heels; she seized the king's wrist with one hand, snatched up her bundle with the other, and began to pour out abuse upon the boy.

The king struggled in the woman's grasp, and cried out:

"Unhand me, you foolish creature; it was not I that stole your goods."

The crowd closed around the king and began calling him names; a brawny blacksmith made a reach for him, saying he would trounce him well, for a lesson; but just then a long sword flashed in the air and, flat-side down, knocked the man's arm.

"One moment, good souls," said wonderful Miles Hendon, "let us proceed gently, not with bad feeling and harsh words. This is matter for the law. Loose your hold from the boy, good woman."

The woman let go, and the king sprang to his deliverer's side, exclaiming, "You have been slow to find me, but you have come at a good time now, Sir Miles."

The crowd fell apart to admit a constable, who approached and was about to lay his hand upon the king's shoulder, when Hendon said, "Gently, good friend, withhold your hand—he shall go peaceably; I am responsible for that. Lead on, we will follow."

The officer led, with the woman and her bundle; Miles and the king followed after, with the crowd at their heels. The king was inclined to rebel; but Hendon said to him in a low voice:

"Think, sire—your laws come from your own royalty; shall their source resist them, yet require his subjects to respect them?"

"You are right; say no more; you shall see that whatever the king of England requires a subject to suffer under the law, he will himself suffer while he holds the station of a subject."

When the woman was called upon to testify before the justice of the peace, she swore that the small prisoner at the bar was the person who had committed the theft; there was no one able to show the contrary, so the king stood convicted. The bundle was now unrolled, and the contents proved to be a plump little roast pig. The judge asked the woman, "What do you hold this property to be worth?"

"Three shillings and eightpence, your worship."

The justice glanced around upon the crowd, then nodded to the constable and said, "Clear the court and close the doors."

It was done. None remained but the two officials, the accused, the accuser, and Miles Hendon. The judge turned to the woman again, and said, "'Tis a poor, ignorant lad, and perhaps was driven hard by hunger. Good woman! Do you know that when one steals a thing worth above the value of thirteen pence ha'penny the law says he shall *hang* for it?"

The little king started, wide-eyed. The woman sprang to her feet, shaking with fright, and cried out, "Oh, my goodness, what have I done! God-a-mercy, I would not

Miles Hendon threw his arms around the king.

hang the poor thing for the whole world! What shall I do?"

The justice said, "Doubtless it is allowable to revise the value, since it is not yet written upon the record."

"Then in God's name, call the pig eighteenpence!"

Miles Hendon threw his arms around the king and hugged him. The woman made her goodbyes and started away with her pig; and when the constable opened the door for her, he followed her out into the narrow hall. Hendon slipped softly into the dusky hall and listened. He heard the constable say, "It is a fat pig, and promises good eating. I will buy it from you; here is eighteenpence."

"Eighteenpence, indeed! You'll do no such thing. It cost me three shillings and eighteenpence. A fig for your eighteenpence!"

"You were under oath, and so swore falsely when you said the value was but eighteenpence. Come right away back with me before his worship, and answer for the crime!—and then the lad will hang!"

"There, there, say no more. Give me the eighteenpence, and hold your peace."

The woman went off crying; Hendon slipped back into the court-room, and the constable soon followed, after hiding his prize in some secret place. The justice was reading the king a wise and kindly lecture, and sentenced him to a short imprisonment in the common jail, to be followed by a public flogging. The astounded king opened his mouth and was probably going to order the good judge to be beheaded on the spot; but he caught a warning sign from Hendon, and succeeded in closing his mouth. They then departed after the constable toward the jail. The moment the street was reached, the angry monarch halted, and exclaimed to Hendon, "You idiot! Do you imagine I will enter a common jail?"

Hendon bent down and said, somewhat sharply, "Will

you trust me? Peace, and try not to worsen our chances with dangerous words."

The short winter day was almost ended. The streets were deserted, save for a few random stragglers. Edward the Sixth wondered if the spectacle of a king on his way to jail had ever encountered such indifference before. By and by the constable arrived at a deserted market-square and proceeded to cross it. When he had reached the middle of it, Hendon laid his hand upon his arm, and said in a low voice, "Wait a moment, good sir."

"Please, do not hinder me."

"Wait, nevertheless, for the matter concerns you. Turn your back a moment and seem not to see; let this poor lad escape."

"You dare say this to me! I arrest you in—"

"No, be not too hasty. The pig you have purchased for eightpence may cost you your neck, man!"

The poor constable, taken by surprise, was speechless.

Hendon said, "I like you, friend, and would not like to see you come to harm. I heard it all between you and the good woman—every word."

"'Tis making a mighty matter indeed, out of a joke!"

"You kept the woman's pig as a joke?"

"Yes! I tell you 'twas a joke."

"By taking advantage of the woman, you have seized good worth above thirteen pence ha'penny; and this, in the eye of the law, is a crime with penalty of death."

"Be merciful," cried the constable. "Spare me this doom, and I will turn my back and see nothing that shall happen."

"Good! Now you are wise and reasonable. And you'll restore the pig to the woman?"

"I will!"

A half an hour later, Hendon and the king were far eastward, riding along on the knight's old horses. The king was warm and comfortable now, for he had clothed himself in a second-hand suit Hendon had bought for him.

When they had journeyed about ten miles, they reached a considerable village, and halted there for the night. Hendon stood behind the king's chair while he dined; undressed him when he was ready for bed; then took the floor for his own, and slept against the door, rolled up in a blanket.

The next day, and the next day after, they jogged lazily along, talking over the adventures they had met since their separation. Hendon detailed all his wide wanderings in search of the king.

During the last day of the trip, Hendon's spirits were soaring. He talked about his old father, and his brother Arthur, and told of many things which illustrated their good characters. He was so happy, he was able to say some gentle things of his wicked brother Hugh.

It was a fair region, dotted with cottages and orchards, and the road led through broad pasture-lands, marked with gentle little hills. At last, Hendon cried out, "There is the village, my prince, and there is Hendon Hall close by! You may see the towers from here; and that wood there—that is my father's park."

All possible hurry was made; still, it was after three o'clock before they arrived at the noble mansion.

"Welcome to Hendon Hall, my king!" exclaimed Miles. "Ah, 'tis a great day! When my father and my brother and the Lady Edith see me, they will be mad with joy."

The next moment, Hendon sprang to the ground from his horse, helped the king down from his, then took him by the hand and rushed inside. A few steps brought him to a large room; he seated the king, then ran toward a young man who sat at a writing table.

"Embrace me, Hugh," he cried, "and say you're glad I am come again! And call our father, for home is not

Hendon took him by the hand and rushed inside.

home till I shall touch his hand, and see his face, and hear his voice once more!"

But Hugh only drew back, and stared at his brother. He said, "Your mind seems mad, poor stranger; doubtless you have suffered at the world's hands; your looks and clothing show that. Whom do you take me to be?"

"Take you to be? For whom else! I take you to be Hugh Hendon."

"And whom do you imagine yourself to be?"

"Imagination has nothing to do with it! Do you pretend you do not know me as your brother Miles Hendon?"

"My brother died in battle six or seven years ago."

"A lie! Call our father—he will know me."

"One may not call the dead."

"Dead? Our father is dead!—oh, this is heavy news. Half my joy is gone now. Then, please, let me see my brother Arthur—he will know me."

"He, also, is dead."

"Gone—both gone—the worthy taken and the worthless spared! Ah, do not say the Lady Edith—"

"Is dead? No, she lives."

"Then my joy is whole again! Let her come to me! She will not say I am not myself."

And so Hugh left the room. Miles walked back and forth, muttering to himself.

The king spoke up, "There are others in the world whose identity is denied, and whose claims are made fun of. You have company in me."

"I am no imposter," cried Hendon. "Here was I born and bred, my lord; I speak the truth. I pray to you not to doubt me—I could not bear it."

"I do not doubt you," said the king. "Do you doubt me, that I am king of England?"

Now, Hendon did, of course, doubt the boy, but luckily, before he had to answer, Hugh and a beautiful lady entered the room.

Miles sprang forward, crying out, "Oh, my Edith, my darling—"

But Hugh waved him back, and said to the lady, "Look at him. Do you know him?"

"I do not know him," she said, turning with a moan and a sob, and quickly leaving the room.

Miles sank into a chair, and covered his face with his hands.

"You have seen that my wife did not know you," said Hugh.

"Your *wife!*" cried Miles. "Oh, you fox-hearted brother, I see it all now! You have stolen my bride and my mansion!"

At this moment, officers burst into the room, and a violent struggle began; but Miles was soon overpowered and dragged away. The king was taken also, and both were tied up and led to prison.

In their cell, the king was furious, and Hendon was bewildered, not understanding how this had all come about.

In the cell next to theirs, an old man, recognizing Hendon, dropped on his knees and whispered, "God be thanked; you're come home again, my master! I believed you were dead these seven years, and lo, here you are alive!"

Miles knew the man, Andrews, and said, "But what has happened in my father's home?"

Little by little, in a whisper, for Andrews did not want to be punished by Sir Hugh Hendon for revealing secrets, the story of the family came out. Arthur had been dead six years. This loss, with the lack of news from Hendon, ruined the father's health; Sir Richard believed he was going to die, and he wished to see Hugh and Edith married before he passed away; but Edith begged for a delay, hoping for Miles's return; then a letter came which brought the news of Miles's death; this shocking news put Sir Richard on his death-bed;

the marriage then took place by the death-bed, and shortly after Sir Richard died. The marriage had not been happy.

Finally, there was a bit of gossip which the king listened to with interest:

"There is rumor that the king is mad."

His majesty glared at the old man and said, "The king is *not* mad, good man!"

Andrews, surprised, said to Hendon, "What does the lad mean?" Hendon gave him a sign to pay no attention to the crazed boy, and so Andrews went on: "The late king is to be buried at Windsor in a day or two—and the new king will be crowned at Westminster a few days later."

"I think they must find the king first!" muttered his majesty.

Andrews was again confused by the boy, but continued, "Sir Hugh goes to the coronation."

"A coronation without a king!" cried his majesty.

"Without a king?" said Andrews. "We have one—his most sacred majesty King Edward the Sixth! Yes, and a dear and gracious little one he is, too; and whether he is mad or not—and they say he gets better daily—all praise him. He is bent on destroying the cruelest of the laws that oppress the people."

This news struck his majesty dumb with amazement. He wondered if the "little one" was the beggar-boy whom he left dressed in his own garments in the palace. It did not seem possible that this could be, for surely his manners and speech would betray him if he pretended to be the Prince of Wales—then he would be driven out, and search made for the true prince. His impatience to get to London grew hourly, and his captivity became almost unendurable.

One morning the jailer came in and commanded that the prisoners be conducted to the jail-yard. The king was overjoyed—it would be a blessed thing to see the blue sky and breathe the fresh air once more. Once there, he conversed with some of the other prisoners, and the tales of their woes wrung his heart. One of them was a poor half-witted woman who had stolen some cloth—she was to be hanged for it. Another man was accused of killing a deer in the king's park, and now he was on his way to the gallows.

The king was furious over these inhumanities, and wanted Hendon to hurry with him to Westminster, so that he could mount his throne and hold out his scepter in mercy over these people and save their lives.

"Poor child," sighed Hendon to himself, "these woeful tales have brought his madness upon him again."

The king went on to say, "No one believes in me—that I am king. But no matter—within a month the laws that have dishonored us, and shamed the English name, shall be swept from the law-books. Kings should go and learn about their own laws at times."

Meantime Miles's trial came on, and he was sentenced to sit two hours in the pillory for being a "sturdy vagabond" and for attacking the master of Hendon Hall.

The king had nearly been condemned to the stocks himself, for being in such bad company, but had been let off with a lecture and a warning, in consideration of his youth. But even so, King Edward was furious to see his poor servant in the stocks, teased and degraded by a dirty mob. He saw an egg sail through the air and crush itself against Hendon's cheek, and heard the crowd roar its enjoyment. The king sprang to the officer in charge, crying:

"For shame! This is my servant—set him free! I am the—"

"Oh, peace!" exclaimed Hendon, "you'll destroy yourself. Don't mind him, officer, he is crazy."

He was sentenced to sit two hours in the pillory.

"I won't mind him," said the officer, "but I'll teach him something." He turned to another soldier and said, "Give the little fool a taste or two of the lash, to mend his manners."

"Half a dozen will better teach him," suggested Sir Hugh, who had ridden up a moment before to watch.

"Let the child go," cried Hendon. "You heartless dogs, don't you see how young and weak he is? Let him go—I will take his lashes."

"Yes, a good thought—and thanks for it," said Sir Hugh. "Let the little beggar go, and give this fellow a dozen in his place."

The king was about to protest, but Sir Hugh silenced him with this remark: "Yes, speak up, do—only for each word you utter he shall get six more strokes."

Hendon was removed from the stocks, and his back laid bare; and while the lash was applied, the poor little king turned away his face and wept.

When the lashing was over, the king went and picked up the whip from the ground, touched Hendon's bleeding shoulders lightly with it, and whispered, "Edward of England dubs thee earl!"

When Hendon's term in the stocks was finished, he was released, and told never to return to the village that was rightfully his own. He and the king rode away on a donkey and a mule—to London!

The whole journey was made without an adventure of importance. But it ended with one. About ten o'clock on the night of the nineteenth of February, they stepped upon London Bridge, in the midst of a traffic jam of howling and hurrahing people. The festivities of the morrow—Coronation Day—were already beginning; everybody was full of strong drink. Within five minutes of the king and Hendon's arrival on the bridge, a fight broke out into a riot. And in this riot, Hendon and the king were hopelessly separated from each other and lost in the rush of the roaring masses of humanity. And so we leave them.

Chapter 10

Tom's Progress

WHILE THE TRUE king wandered about the land, poorly dressed, poorly fed, roughed up and mocked by tramps, herding with thieves and murderers in a jail, and called idiot and imposter by all, the mock king Tom Canty enjoyed quite a different experience.

When we saw him last, royalty was just beginning to have a bright side for him. He soon lost his fears about what to do; he now had an easy and confident manner.

He came to enjoy being conducted to bed at night, and dressed with ceremony in the morning. It came to be a pleasure to march to dinner attended by officers and gentlemen. He liked to hear the bugles sounding down the long corridors, and the distant voices responding, "Make way for the king!"

He even learned to enjoy sitting on a throne. He liked receiving great ambassadors, and listening to the affectionate messages they brought him from other monarchs who called him "brother." Oh, happy Tom Canty of Offal Court!

He enjoyed his splendid clothes, and ordered more. However, he remained kind and gentle, and he made a tireless war upon unjust laws.

Did Tom never feel troubled about the poor little rightful prince who had treated him so kindly, and flown out with such anger to avenge him upon the rude guard at the palace gate? Yes; his first royal days and nights were full of painful thoughts about the lost prince, and he had sincerely longed for his return. But as time wore on, and the prince did not come, Tom's mind became more and more occupied with his new and enchanting experiences, and little by little the vanished monarch faded almost out of his thoughts.

At midnight of the nineteenth of February, Tom Canty was sinking to sleep in his rich bed in the palace, guarded by his loyal soldiers. Tomorrow was the day appointed for his solemn crowning as king of England. At that same hour, Edward, the true king, hungry and thirsty, dirty and worn with travel, and clothed in rags—a result of the riot—was wedged in among a crowd of people who were watching with deep interest gangs of workmen who streamed in and out of Westminster Abbey, busy as ants; they were making the last preparations for the royal coronation.

The next morning, Tom Canty, splendidly clothed, mounted a prancing war-horse, and set out in procession from the palace through the streets of London. The King's Guard formed in single ranks on either side, clad in armor.

To all in the crowds that wished him well, he gave thanks. to such as said "God save his Grace," he said in return, "God save you all!" and added that he thanked them with all his heart.

Finally, the people burst forth in a glad shout, "God preserve you, we pray, and wish you ever well!"

Tom gazed over the surging sea of eager faces, and his heart swelled with pride. He felt that the one thing worth living for in this world was to be a king, and a nation's idol. Soon, he caught sight, at a distance, of a

Tom mounted a prancing war-horse.

couple of his ragged Offal Court friends. Oh, if they could only recognize him now! What glory it would be, if they realized that the boy of the slums and back alleys had become a real king, with dukes and princes for his servants, and the English world at his feet!

Every now and then rose the cry, "A gift! a gift!" and Tom responded by tossing a handful of bright new coins for the crowd to scramble for.

The great parade moved on, and still on, under one triumphal arch after another, and past numerous banners and streamers.

"And all these wonders and these marvels are to welcome me—me!" murmured Tom.

At one point, just as he was raising his hand to fling another handful of coins, he caught sight of a pale, astounded face which was strained forward, its intense eyes upon him. He recognized his mother! In an instant she had torn her way out of the crowd, and past the guards, and was at his side. She embraced his leg, she covered it with kisses, she cried, "Oh, my child, my darling!" lifting toward him a joyful, loving face.

"I do not know you," said Tom, and a guard snatched her away, and brought her back to the crowd. A shame fell upon Tom which withered his pride.

The procession moved on, and still on, through ever more splendors and welcomes; but to Tom Canty they were as if they had not been. He neither saw nor heard. Royalty had lost its grace and sweetness. He was eating his heart out with shame for having disavowed his mother.

But at last he and his train of guardsmen and dukes and princes arrived at Westminster Abbey. While Tom was being prepared and robed, the greatest officials of the land filed onto the gorgeous platform inside.

There was a waiting pause; then, at a signal, a triumphant peal of music burst forth, and Tom Canty, clothed in a long robe of gold, appeared at a door, and stepped upon the platform. The entire multitude rose, and the ceremony of Recognition came.

Then a noble piece of music swept through the Abbey; and thus greeted, Tom Canty was conducted to the throne. At last the final act was at hand. The Archbishop of Canterbury lifted up the crown of England from its cushion and held it out over the trembling mock king's head.

A deep hush went over the Abbey. At this impressive moment, a startling figure intruded upon the scene—a figure observed by no one in the absorbed crowd, until it suddenly appeared, moving up the great central aisle. It was a boy, bareheaded, clothed in rags. He raised his hand, and delivered these words of warning:

"I forbid you to set the crown of England upon that head. *I* am the king!"

In an instant, several hands were laid upon the boy; but in the same instant, Tom Canty, in his regal clothes, made a swift step forward and cried, "Let him go! He *is* the king!"

A sort of panic swept the assemblage, and they rose in their places and stared at one another and at the chief figures in this scene, like persons who wondered whether they were awake and in their senses, or asleep and dreaming.

The hands were taken away; no one moved, no one spoke. The boy moved steadily forward now; he stepped upon the platform, and the mock king ran with a glad face to meet him, and fell upon his knees before him and said, "O, my lord the king, let poor Tom Canty be first to swear loyalty to you, and say, 'Put on your crown!'"

The great officers upon the platform looked on and thought, "What a strange resemblance!"

The Lord Protector, the Duke of Somerset, came forward and said to the true king, "By your favor, sir, I desire to ask certain questions which—"

A startling figure intruded upon the scene.

"I will answer them, my lord."

The duke asked him many questions about the court, the late king, the prince, the princesses. The boy answered them correctly and without hesitating. He

described the rooms in the palace, the late king's apart-
ments, and those of the Prince of Wales.

But the Duke of Somerset shook his head and said, "It
is surprising that you know so much, and yet it is no
more than our lord the king likewise can do. These are
not proofs." Then the duke remembered an important
question: "Where is the Great Seal? Answer this; for
only he that was Prince of Wales can answer it!"

Yes, no one but the true prince could solve the mys-
tery of the vanished Great Seal.

But, no, the king-in-rags could not remember.

The duke wondered aloud, "How can so bulky a thing
as the Seal of England vanish away and no man be able
to get track of it again—a large golden disk—"

Tom Canty sprang forward and shouted, "That's it!
Was it round?—and thick?—and did it have letters and
designs engraved upon it?—Yes? Oh, *now* I know what
this Great Seal is that there's been such a worry about!
If you had described it to me, you could have had it
three weeks ago. I know where it lies; but it was not I
that put it there—first."

"Who, then, my lord?" asked the duke.

"He that stands there—the rightful king of England.
And he shall tell you himself where it lies—then you
will believe he knew it of his own knowledge. Think, my
king—spur your memory—it was the last, the very last
thing you did that day before you rushed out of the
palace, clothed in my rags, to punish the soldier that
insulted me."

All eyes were fixed upon the newcomer, who stood,
with head bent, groping in his memory for one single
little fact, which found, would seat him upon the
throne—unfound, would leave him as he was—a pauper and an outcast. Moment after moment passed—

still the boy struggled silently on, and gave no sign. But at last he heaved a sigh, shook his head slowly, and said, with a trembling lip, "I call the scene back—all of it—but the Seal has no place in it." He paused, then looked up, and said, "My lords and gentlemen, if you will rob your rightful king of his own for lack of this evidence, I may not stop you, but—"

"Wait, my king!" cried Tom Canty, "wait!—think! Do not give up! Listen to what I say—follow every word—I am going to bring that morning back again, just as it happened. We talked—I told you of my sisters, Nan and Bet—ah, yes, you remember that; and about my old grandmother—and the rough games of the lads of Offal Court—yes, you remember these things also; very well, follow me still. You gave me food and drink—ah, yes, this also you remember."

As Tom checked off his details, and the other boy nodded his head, the great audience and the officials stared in wonder; the tale sounded true, yet how could this impossible meeting between a prince and a pauper have come about?

"For a jest, my prince," continued Tom, "we exchanged garments. Then we stood before a mirror; and so alike were we that both said it seemed as if there had been no change made—yes, you remember that. Then you noticed that the soldier had hurt my hand— look! here it is. At this your highness sprang up, vowing vengeance upon the soldier, and ran toward the door— you passed a table—that thing you call the Seal lay on that table—you snatched it up and looked eagerly about, as if for a place to hide it—your eye caught sight of—"

"There, 'tis enough!—and dear God be thanked!" exclaimed the king. "Go, my good St. John—in an arm-piece of the armor that hangs on the wall, you'll find the Seal!"

"Right, my king! Right!" cried Tom Canty; "now the scepter of England is your own!—Go, my Lord St. John, give your feet wings!"

The whole assemblage was on its feet now, and almost out of its mind with uneasiness and excitement. On the floor and on the platform a deafening buzz of conversation burst forth. At last a sudden hush fell upon the house, and in the same moment St. John appeared upon the platform and held the Great Seal high in his hand. Then such a shout went up!

"Long live the true king!"

For five minutes the air quaked with shouts and the crash of musical instruments, and was white with a storm of waving handkerchiefs; and through it all a ragged lad stood, happy and proud, in the center of the platform, with the great lords of the kingdom kneeling around him.

Then all rose, and Tom Canty cried out, "Now, O my king, take these regal garments back, and give poor Tom, your servant, his rags again."

The Lord Protector spoke up: "Let the small rascal be stripped and flung into the Tower!"

But the new king, the true king, said, "I will not have it so. If not for him I would not have got my crown again—none shall lay a hand upon him to harm him. As for you, my good uncle, my Lord Protector, this conduct of yours is not grateful toward this poor lad, for I hear he had made you a duke"—the Protector blushed—"yet he was not a king; and so, what is your fine title worth now? Tomorrow you shall ask me, through his consent, for its confirmation, or else no duke, but a simple earl, shall you remain."

The king turned to Tom, and said, kindly, "My poor boy, how was it that you could remember where I hid the Seal when I could not remember it myself?"

"Ah, my king, that was easy, since I used it several times."

St. John held the Great Seal high in his hand.

"Used it—yet could not explain where it was?"

"I did not know it was *that* they wanted. They did not describe it, your majesty."

"Then how did you use it?"

"To crack nuts with!"

Poor child, the flood of laughter that greeted this nearly swept him off his feet.

Meanwhile, the rich robe had been removed from Tom's shoulders to the king's, whose rags were hidden from sight under it. Then the coronation ceremonies were resumed; the true king was anointed and the crown set upon his head, while cannon thundered the news to the city, and all London seemed to rock with applause.

Chapter 11

Edward as King

MILES HENDON had had little money when the riot started on London Bridge, and none at all when he got out. The pickpockets had stripped him of his last farthing.

But that did not matter to him, if he found the boy. So Miles started on his quest. Hour after hour he tramped through the back alleys and dirty streets. He had no luck. When evening came he lay down on the ground under a hedge and rested. A faint, far-off boom of cannon came to his ear, and he said to himself, "The new king is crowned," and fell asleep. He had not slept or rested for more than thirty hours. He did not wake again until the middle of the next morning. He set off for the king's palace; he meant to explain to the good young king, or more likely one of his lords, why Hendon Hall ought to be returned to him.

Toward eleven o'clock he approached the palace. The king's whipping-boy, who had been so useful for Tom's education in kingliness, passed by Hendon, then wheeled about and scanned his figure well, saying to himself, "If that is not the very wanderer his majesty is in such a worry about, then I'm a donkey. He answers the description to a rag." The whipping-boy went up to Hendon and said, "Please, sir, follow me."

"You?"

"Into the palace. You are wanted."

"Indeed!" said an astonished Hendon.

The two walked past guards and gates and arrived at the grand entrance of the palace, where an officer, with a bow, escorted Hendon into the hands of an official, who greeted him with respect, and led him forward through a great hall, lined on both sides with servants, and up a broad staircase, among flocks of fine folk, and finally brought him into a large room, made a passage for him through the assembled nobility of England, then made a bow, reminded Miles to take his hat off, and left him standing in the middle of the room, a mark for all eyes.

Miles Hendon was entirely bewildered. There sat the young king, five steps away, with his head bent down and aside, speaking with a duke. Then the king raised his head slightly and Hendon caught a good view of his face. The sight nearly took his breath away! He stood gazing at the face like one under a spell; then soon exclaimed to himself, "The boy who imagined he was king is on his throne!"

He stared at the king again, who had not yet noticed him—and thought, "Is it a dream? . . . or is he the true king of England, and not the friendless poor lad I took him for—who shall solve for me this riddle?"

A sudden idea flashed in his eye, and he strode to the wall, gathered up a chair, brought it back, planted it on the floor, and sat down in it!

A buzz of anger against him broke out, a rough hand was laid upon him, and a voice exclaimed, "Up, you mannerless clown! Would you sit in the presence of the king?"

He dropped upon his knees and swore allegiance.

The disturbance attracted his majesty's attention who stretched forth his hand and cried out, "Do not touch him, it is his right!"

The crowd fell back. The king went on:

"Know this, all of you, ladies, lords, and gentlemen, that this is my trusty and well-beloved servant, Miles Hendon, who with his good sword saved his prince from bodily harm and possible death—and for this he is a knight, by my wish. Also learn, that he is now a peer of England, Earl of Kent, and shall have gold and lands enough. More—the privilege which he has just demonstrated is his by royal grant; we have ordained that the chiefs of his line shall have and hold the right to sit in the presence of the majesty of England from now on."

"Oh, my!" said Miles, still staring at the king, "this is the one I thought a pauper! This is the lunatic!"

Then his manners came back, and he dropped upon his knees, and swore allegiance to him and his kingdom. Then he rose and stood aside.

Now the king saw amongst the crowd Sir Hugh, Miles's wicked brother, and spoke out, with a wrathful voice, "Strip this robber of his goods and stolen estates, and put him under lock and key."

Then Sir Hugh was led away.

There was a stir at the other end of the room now; the assemblage fell apart, and Tom Canty, richly clothed, marched down, preceded by an usher. He knelt before the king, who said:

"I have learned the story of these past few weeks, and am well pleased with you. You have governed the realm with royal gentleness and mercy. You have found your mother and sisters again? Good; they shall be cared for. Know, all of you, that from this day, the paupers and orphans that live in the shelter of Christ's Hospital shall have their minds and hearts fed, as well as their stomachs; and this boy shall dwell there, and be the chief of its governors. He has the throne's protection, he has the crown's support, and he shall be known and called by the honorable title of the King's Ward."

The proud and happy Tom Canty rose and kissed the king's hand, and was conducted from his presence. He then flew to his mother, to tell her and Nan and Bet all about it and get them to help him enjoy the great news.

Tom lived to be a very old man.

When the mysteries were all cleared up, it came out, by confession of Hugh Hendon, that his wife had, by his command, pretended not to know Miles that day at Hendon Hall. Hugh now deserted his wife and went over to France, where he soon died; and by and by the Earl of Kent, our Miles, married his Edith.

Tom Canty's father was never heard of again.

As long as the king lived he was fond of telling the story of his adventures, all through, from the hour that the guard knocked him away from the palace gate, till the final midnight, when he joined a gang of hurrying workmen and so slipped into the Abbey and climbed up and hid himself in a tomb, and then slept till the next day.

Miles Hendon and Tom Canty were favorites of the king, all through his brief life, and mourned him when he died.

Tom lived to be a very old man, a handsome, white-haired fellow. As long as he lasted he was honored; whenever he appeared in public the crowd fell apart, making way for him, and whispering, "Tip your hat, it is the King's Ward!"—and so they saluted, and got his kindly smile in return.

Yes, King Edward VI lived only a few years, poor boy, but he lived them worthily. More than once, when some great lord made an argument against his kindness to his subjects or against the gentle amendments Edward called for in the severe laws, the young king turned his eyes upon him and answered:

"What do you know of suffering and oppression? I and my people know, but not you."

The reign of Edward VI was a merciful one for those harsh times. Now that we are taking leave of him let us try to keep this in our minds, to his credit.